Ken Bruen was born in Galway, Ireland. After turning down a place at RADA, and completing a doctorate in Metaphysics, he spent twenty-five years as an English teacher in Africa, Japan, South-East Asia and South America. An unscheduled stint in a Brazilian prison where he suffered physical and mental abuse spurred him to write and, after a brief spell teaching in London, he returned to Galway, where he now lives with his daughter.

Ken Bruen is the award-winning author of nine Jack Taylor novels, four of which have now been filmed for an acclaimed TV3 series starring Iain Glen in the eponymous role. Ken has also written a number of standalone novels, two of which were released as films recently – *London Boulevard* (starring Keira Knightley and Colin Farrell) and *Blitz* (starring Jason Statham).

For more information on Ken Bruen and his books, see his website at www.kenbruen.com

www.transworldbooks.co.uk

www.transworldireland.ie

Also by Ken Bruen

FUNERAL

SHADES OF GRACE

MARTYRS

RILKE ON BLACK

THE HACKMAN BLUES

HER LAST CALL TO LOUIS MACNEICE

A WHITE ARREST

TAMING THE ALIEN

THE MCDEAD

LONDON BOULEVARD

BLITZ

VIXEN

The Jack Taylor novels

THE GUARDS

THE KILLING OF THE TINKERS

THE MAGDALEN MARTYRS

THE DRAMATIST

PRIEST

CROSS

SANCTUARY

THE DEVIL

HEADSTONE

KEN BRUEN

Headstone

A Jack Taylor Novel

TRANSWORLD IRELAND

TRANSWORLD IRELAND
An imprint of The Random House Group Limited
20 Vauxhall Bridge Road, London SW1V 2SA
www.transworldbooks.co.uk

HEADSTONE
A TRANSWORLD IRELAND BOOK: 9781848271180

First published in 2012 by Transworld Ireland
a division of Transworld Publishers
Transworld Ireland paperback edition published 2013

Addresses for Random House Group Ltd companies outside the UK
can be found at: www.randomhouse.co.uk
The Random House Group Ltd Reg. No. 954009

The Random House Group Limited supports The Forest Stewardship Council® (FSC®),
the leading international forest-certification organisation. Our books carrying the FSC
label are printed on FSC®-certified paper. FSC is the only forest-certification scheme
supported by the leading environmental organisations, including Greenpeace. Our paper
procurement policy can be found at www.randomhouse.co.uk/environment

Typeset in Sabon by Falcon Oast Graphic Art Ltd.
Printed and bound by CPI Group (UK) Ltd, Croydon, CR0 4YY.

2 4 6 8 10 9 7 5 3 1

Philip Spitzer, agent extraordinaire
Lukas Ortiz, *mi hermano*
Joel Gotler, the Wizard
Renate Hutton, who, wonderfully, buys the books

Prologue

He drained the last of the pint, thought,

'*Christ, that was good.*'

Another Jay?

Tempting?

Phew-oh.

But he'd had two alongside the batter of pints already. Primarily, he needed a cig.

That tipped the balance. He could already feel the first hit of ferocious nicotine.

He moved from his stool, brushed the dandruff from his jacket. Normally he didn't notice it, but he'd caught sight of himself in the old mirror with the slogan MY GOODNESS, MY GUINNESS and a frazzled comic zookeeper chasing a pelican with pints of the black in his beak. Nearly made him smile; you just didn't see those ancient slogans any more. More's the Irish pity. He cursed anew those damn black jackets that showed up every fleck of white. Like stranded drops of snow. He said,

''Night all.'

Got a few muttered 'God bless'es.

No warmth though.

Fecking media had given his profession the taint of leprosy. Grudgingly, he conceded that not paying for any of his drinks the whole evening might be a factor.

He thought,

'*Bad cess to ye.*'

Outside, he stared at the church. St Nicholas's. One of the two Protestant outfits in the city. They claimed some hoof-marks inside the door were made by Christopher Columbus before he set sail to find the New World. He figured they needed all the lures they could conjure. He got out his pack of Major, the strongest Irish cigarette – none of that Marlboro Light shite for him. Smoke or fuck off. He wouldn't be surprised if the decaffeinated-tea rumour was true.

Flicked his Bic.

Got the first lethal drags of smoke into his starved lungs.

When the blow came to the back of his skull,

hard,

he dropped the cig, nearly fell. Then a massive kick to his stomach brought him to his knees. The mix of Jameson and Guinness spewed forth like a nervous confession. He heard,

'Fucking bastard's spewing.'

Another forceful kick laid him flat on his back. He could barely see, had the mad thought,

'*Nothing good happens outside a Prod church.*'

Though he could barely see from pain, he registered three figures. Was one a girl? He heard,

'He's wearing his dog collar.'

And it was ripped from his neck with the chant of

'Woof-woof.'

A hand in his jacket, ripping out his wallet. Holding it up for the others to see, a male voice going,

'He's got a photo in here.'

The chorus,

'Who is it then? Britney? Lindsay Lohan?'

An answer.

'Some old cunt.'

His mother.

He made the drastic mistake of trying to get up; surely the young people still had some respect?

Right.

The next kick broke his nose.

He fell back.

The girl stood over him, sneered,

'Trying to see up my skirt, yah pervert?'

And shredded the photo into his face. She paused, added,

'Nearly forgot this.'

Spat in his face.

He heard,

'Who's for a pint then?'

As they moved away, he allowed himself a tiny flicker of hope, till one hesitated, came back and, with slow and deadly aim, kicked him in the side of his head and laughed.

'Forgive me, Father, for *you* have sinned.'

A light rain began to fall, drenching what remained of his

mother's torn photo. She'd always wanted him to be a priest. As his eyes rolled back into his head, he muttered, 'Top of the world, Ma.'

1

'A headstone is but a slab of granite lashed by an indifferent wind.'

Caz, Romanian domiciled in Galway

Things were looking up. Late October had brought a week of Indian summer. Was it global warming, the world going to hell?

Who cared?

We grabbed it while it lasted.

Eyre Square, people lying out in the sunshine. Ice-cream vendors peddling slush at five euro a pop. The country had on a second referendum said *yes* to the Lisbon Treaty. We took that for what it was . . .

A brief stay from Death Row.

I was coming off the worst case of my bedraggled career. Literally, a brush with the Devil. I muttered,

'Darkness visible.'

Had sworn,

'Never, never going down that dark path again.'

Whatever it was,

the Occult,

devilment,

Xanax,

delusion,

it had shaken me to the core. I still kept the lights on in the wee hours, in my apartment in, get this, Nun's Island.

Who said God had no sense of the ridiculous?

To add bemusement to bafflement, I'd met a woman. After the Devil, I'd gone to London on one of those late-deal internet offers. Met Laura. An American, aged forty-two, and, to me,

gorgeous.

She made my heart skip a beat. She was a writer of crime fiction. At my most cynical, I thought I was simply material for her next book. A broken-down Irish PI, with a limp and a hearing aid.

Yeah, that would fly.

Did I care?

Did I fuck.

She liked me.

I grabbed that like the last beads of the rosary. She had rented a house in Notting Hill and was due to come and stay with me for a week. But hedging our collective bets, we went to Paris for five days, to see if there was any real substance in what we thought we had. February in that wondrous city. Should have been cold and bitter.

Nope.

Such gods there are gave us the Moveable Feast. Glorious freak spring weather. We had a lovely hotel close to the Irish Institute and were but a *bonjour* from the Luxembourg Gardens, where we spent most of our time. I was nervous as a cat, so long since I'd been in bed with a woman – a woman

I hadn't paid for, that is. My scarred body, I dreaded she would be repulsed by it. The opposite, she seemed to embrace my hurt and pain. Whispered as she ran her fingers along one lengthy scar,

'No more beatings, Jack, OK?'

Worked for me.

In Hemingway's beautiful memoir, he writes of the miraculous time he and his wife had and how they felt it would last for ever. And wood was all around them and he never touched it for luck. I said that to Laura, she answered,

'You touched my heart, that's all the luck we need.'

Would it were so.

Sweet Jesus.

I'd sworn that despite the French and their customs, you'd never catch me eating food in the park. I'd never be uninhibited enough to grab a roll and eat it as I lay on the grass.

I did, loved it – a bottle of Nuits Saint Georges, amazing French sandwiches, wedges of cheese, the almost warm sunshine and Laura. Jesus, it was heaven. I even rolled up my shirtsleeves. Made her laugh out loud. She said,

'My God, you heathen, you.'

Like that.

We did all the tourist crap and relished it. Got our photograph taken on Boulevard Saint Michel. I carry the photo in my wallet and never, never look at it now. I can't. But it's there, like the blessing I once believed I'd been granted. Went to the Louvre and made her laugh again when I said the Mona Lisa was little more than a postage stamp.

In Montmartre on the second-last day of our holiday, drinking café au lait in an early-morning bistro, she reached across the table, took my hand for reasons none at all, said,

'You make me happy.'

Jesus, *mon Dieu*, me, making anyone happy. I was fit to burst.

Our last evening, in a restaurant on the Left Bank, she literally fed me escargots and I thought,

'*Fuck, if they could see me in Galway now.*'

And then her idea:

'Jack, if my next book deal comes through, would you consider living here for six months?'

Was she kidding? I'd have stayed there right then.

In bed that night, after slow lingering lovemaking, we were entwined in each other and she asked,

'Are you content to be with me, Jack?'

I told the truth:

'More than my bedraggled heart could ever have imagined.'

After, when I got home and we were arranging for Laura to come to Galway, I went to the church, lit a candle, pleaded,

'I've never asked for much, but if it doesn't screw with some inflexible divine plan, could I please have this woman with me, could Paris be indeed a Moveable Feast?'

And the candle flickered, went out.

An omen?

Maybe.

My drinking. She was aware of it, Jesus, how could

she not be? But she seemed to think there was hope.

I abetted the illusion. No doubt I'd fuck it up. Sure as the granite on the walls of Galway Cathedral. But if this were my one last day in the sun, then I intended to bask.

My odd-times friend/accomplice/conscience was Stewart. A former drug-dealer who'd reinvented himself as a Zen-spouting entrepreneur. He'd saved my life on more than one occasion. I was never sure if he actually liked me, but I sure as fuck intrigued him.

I could hear strains of Loreena McKennitt carried on the light breeze from somebody's radio. Worked for me, till my mobile shrilled.

I answered, heard,

'Jack?'

'Yeah?'

'It's Stewart.'

Before I could snap off some pithy rejoinder, he said,

'Malachy has been badly hurt.'

Father Malachy, bane of my life. Close confidant of my late mother, he despised me almost as much as I despised myself. Stewart still clung to the notion that I could be redeemed. Malachy believed I had no future and my present was pretty much fucked too. His ingrained hatred of me was fuelled by the fact that I'd once saved his clerical arse. He could have been the poster boy for 'No good deed goes unpunished.'

But I took no joy in him being hurt, unless I was the one who did the hurting. He was part of my shrinking history and I clung to the battered remnants like an early-morning wino and his last drops of rotgut.

I asked,

'How?'

Pause.

Stewart was trying to phrase it as delicately as he could, gave up, said,

'He was mugged.'

I nearly went,

'But he's a priest.'

The awful fact wasn't that priests were mugged in our shiny new country, it was that more weren't.

Stewart said that Malachy was in UCHG, the University Hospital, in Intensive Care. I said I'd get up there straight away. He said, hesitantly,

'Ah Jack, go easy.'

Then a thought hit me.

Hard.

Steel in my voice, I asked,

'You think I did it?'

'Of course not.'

I eased, said,

'Well, least you think I have some standards.'

He shot back,

'If you mugged him, he wouldn't be in the hospital.'

'What?'

'He'd be in the morgue.'

And he clicked off.

*

Reluctantly, I left Eyre Square. Was it my imagination or was the sun already receding? The recession was in full bite. We'd buried the Celtic Tiger ages ago. The papers carried daily dire forebodings of worse to come. The spectre of emigration was looming all over again.

And yet.

A huge new outlet for TK Maxx had just opened. *'Designer clothes at affordable prices.'* At the Grand Opening a week earlier, people had queued for seven hours beforehand. The line of recession-proof people had stretched from the statue of Liam Mellows, our Republican hero, past Boyles Betting Shop (free coffee for punters!), along Cuba nightclub's pink façade, and of course past the inevitable off-licence (ten cans of Bavarian Lager for ten euros) to the very doors of the new shopping Mecca.

On the great day, a local had invoked St Anthony's brief:

Flee, you hostile powers,

the lion of the tribe of Judah,

the root of David hath conquered . . . Alleluia.

St Anthony wasn't available that day, the only alleluias we were familiar with were mangled versions of Leonard Cohen's classic by *X-Factor* wannabes.

Recession, my arse.

Swine flu continued to stalk, slowly but deadly, across the land. The death toll was higher than the government would admit. But hey, they had good news: we'd only a year to wait for the vaccine.

And just to add a kick in the balls, they said,

'It will be administered according to priorities.'

Meaning the likes of me weren't in the top ten.

I passed down by HMV, who were touting Season Three of *Dexter*, the serial killer who only kills the bad guys.

Maybe we could import him.

Then down past Abrakebabra, the home of the drunkard's beloved late-night kebab. I turned at what used to be Moon's shop and is now the posh Brown Thomas, selling the latest Gucci handbag at the amazing price of only three thousand euros.

I doubt my late dad ever saw three thousand pounds his whole wretched life.

I passed Golden Discs, now closed – the lease had run out – and reached the abbey. Recently renovated, it looked much the same, except the price of a Mass card had sky-rocketed. I dipped my fingers in the Holy Water font, blessed myself and headed for St Anthony's altar. I lit a candle for Malachy and for my legion of dead and departed. At the rate those I knew were dying, I could open my own private cemetery, issue loyalty cards and, why not, air miles.

You want something from St Anthony, it's real simple.

Pay him.

I did.

Shoved a large note in the slot and momentarily was lost for words.

So many dead.

The best and the brightest, as always. I prayed for a little girl, Serena May, who still tore the heart out of my chest.

Back when I'd been trying to find who killed Stewart's sister, I spent a lot of hours with the Down syndrome child of my close friends, Jeff and Cathie. The little girl filled me with wonder and yearning; it was like I felt my life had some meaning. Her gurgle of delight when I read to her did what gallons of Jameson failed to do: it gave me ease. Her terrible death, literally in my presence, was a lament of such horrendous proportions that I had a complete breakdown and was in a mental hospital for months. Some things you never reconcile and Serena May was my daily burden of love and care, crushed beyond all recognition.

I prayed for Cody, my surrogate son, dead because of me.

Back in the time of the Tinkers, I'd taken on a young impressionable kid, one of those wannabe-American young Irish who saw the world through a cinema lens. In the beginning, I'd given him literally errands to run, but over time we'd developed a bond, so that I came to regard him as the son I'd never have. It was a time of richness, of joy, of fulfilment in my shattered life. And what the gods give . . . they sure as fuck take away.

Mercilessly.

He was cut down by a crazed sniper with a hard-on for me.

His loss was a cross I'd never climb down from.

Finally, I asked that I might find a modicum of peace.

2

'It's not what you read, or even study, it's how you bend the material to shape and endorse your own dark designs.'

Caz

The basement was lit by thirteen black candles. A flat slab of granite in the rough design of a headstone was supported by beer crates and acted as a table. Three ordinary kitchen chairs were placed thus:

two on the right side,

one, almost forlorn, on the left.

On top of the table was an ornate throne, rescued from a theatrical shop – like most businesses, gone bust: the throne had been dumped in a skip. It had been cleaned up and now was alight with velvet cushions and a decorative banner, proclaiming THE NEW ORDER.

Behind, pinned on the wall, were:

a massive swastika,

a black and white map of a school,

a worn, battered T-shirt of one of the death-metal groups.

On the right side of the table were two brothers, Jimmy and Sean Bennet. They could have passed as twins but Sean was actually three years older. They both had long black hair that they seemed to take turns in flicking out of their eyes. They came from one of the wealthiest, oldest Galway families and had inherited, aside from shitloads of cash:

arrogance,

entitlement,

deep, seething, malignant resentment.

An Irish version of the Mendoza brothers, but it was unlikely they'd even heard of that infamous duo. Their range of knowledge was limited, like products of all the wealthiest schools. They smoked continuously, Marlboro Red, and had identical Zippos, chunky ones with the logo:

HEADSTONE.

Opposite them was a girl. Currently answering to Bethany. That changed as frequently as her mood. Her current look was Goth: deathly pale face, black mascara, eyeliner, lipstick and, of course, raven hair to her shoulders. As Ruth Rendell titled her novel, *An Unkindness of Ravens*.

She was very pretty beneath all the gunk and she knew it. More, she knew how to use it. She was twenty-three, burning with a rage even she no longer knew the motive for. She had embraced hatred with all the zeal of a zealot and relished the black fuel it provided.

On the throne was Bine.

Older than all of them and so intoxicated by power he never even thought of his real name any more. In front of him was a small bust of Charles Darwin. He had studied the man and completely misunderstood what he'd read.

His crew were dressed as he'd ordered: black sweatshirts,

combat pants and Doc Martens. With metal toes. To his side was a wooden crate containing:

six grenades,

three assault rifles,

a riot of handguns,

eight sticks of gelignite.

Two years – count 'em, two fucking years – of bribery, cajoling, stealing, to assemble that arsenal. They were, he felt, almost ready. He gestured to Bethany, said,

'Drinks.'

Like most raised in a privileged fashion, he had no fucking manners.

A fleeting frown crossed her face, but she rose, fetched the bottle of Wild Turkey, the inevitable bottles of Coke,

'cos everything goes better with it, right?

Brought them to the table, thinking,

'Same old macho bullshit.'

Jimmy, always anxious to please, fetched the heavy Galway crystal tumblers and Bethany poured lethal dollops of the Turkey, with a splatter of Coke, handed the first to Bine.

He raised his, toasted,

'To chaos.'

As was the custom, they near finished the drinks on a first attempt and all managed to stem the 'Holy Fuck' that such a dose of Wild demanded.

Bine, his cheeks aflame, said,

'To business.'

Sean stood.

Once, he'd sat while reporting and Bine had slashed his face with a Stanley knife.

Sean said,

'Attacks: we've hit the old priest and await your next target.'

Bine moved his finger, meaning 'Refills.'

That done, he seemed almost relaxed. He caressed his manifesto. By mangling Darwin, he'd managed to convince them of the urgency of ridding the city of:

the misfits,

the handicapped,

the vulnerable,

the weak,

the pitiful.

Bethany thought it was a crock, but Bine gave her an icy cold channel for her rage, so she acted like she bought into his motives. And though she despised herself, she had such a lust for him she was prepared to go along with whatever frenzy he'd envisaged. It sated her need to lash out alone.

Bine said,

'James?'

Jimmy leaped to attention, went and got the nose candy, a mini headstone with cocaine done in nice consecutive lines, and, presenting a fifty-euro note, offered the gear first to Bine.

He did three lines fast, moved the stuff to Sean, who did the same, followed by Jimmy and, finally, Bethany.

She didn't give a proverbial toss that they were as

chauvinistic as the very society they decried; she did four
lines just to fuck with the system.

She smiled as the dope jolted and at their almost boyish
cries of

'Sweet Jaysus,'

'Darwin rocks,'

'Bring it on, muthahfuckahs.'

She watched Bine carefully, even as she felt the icy dribble
down her own throat. Christ on a bike, that was A-1 dope;
she was in danger of speaking, such was the potency. She
knew the K could take him either way:

magnanimous

or

malevolent.

He caught her stare, asked,

'The knife?'

She produced the new Japanese blade he'd ordered –
serrated edge and as sharp as a bishop avoiding paedo
allegations.

He studied it, asked,

'And this is for whom?'

She bit her tongue, said,

'As you desire.'

Fuck, even to her own self she sounded like a wench in an
Elizabethan drama or, worse, a bad Russell Crowe medieval
romp.

He moved his finger along the edge, letting the fine blade
draw blood, and sucked at it, the blood on his lips. She
knew sex would be rough and violent, and the stupid bollix,

he'd probably bring the knife to bed. Men and their macho toys. He said,

'Mmmm . . . in keeping with our strategy, I want a retard, but I want him gutted. Can you do that?'

She wanted to say,

'*How fucking difficult can it be, killing a handicapped person?*'

Went with,

'When do you want it to happen?'

He smiled. If warmth had ever touched that expression, it had long since fled. He had had his teeth filed down to points, adding to the sardonic effect.

'As soon as you find a suitable dribbling idiot.'

She wanted to say,

'*Have you been in the pubs in Quay Street recently?*'

But irony was not his strong point.

He suddenly leaped to his feet, the Japanese knife curled in his right hand. He said to Sean,

'More drinks, me-finks.'

Sean knew when Bine tried to speak Brit shit was coming down the pike. And hard. He poured the Wild into Bine's tumbler, trying to disguise the tremble in his hand.

Bine began to move down the table, humming 'We Are The Champions'. Stopped behind Jimmy, who began to turn till Bine laid a hand on his shoulder, asked,

'Why does the priest live?'

Almost a metaphysical question.

Before Jimmy could mutter some answer, Bine leaned forward, slashed his cheek from eye to mouth. Blood gushed on to the headstone. Jimmy gasped, raised his hand to stem the flow. Bine said,

'Let it bleed.'

Cue to Bethany, who moved to the sound system, put on 'Exile On Main Street'. As Jagger began to moan and Keith laid on the heavy thump, Bine moved back to the map of the school on the wall, said,

'December Eight, the Feast of the Immaculate Conception, they'll be having their special treat of turkey in the canteen.'

Swung around, eyed his crew, said, as he cackled,

'A turkey shoot.'

3

'God holds unique plans for those who others label handicapped.'

Jeff, dad of Serena May

Tom Reed had been born with Down syndrome.

'Mild,' the doctor had said.

Tess, Tom's mum, nearly screamed,

'Fucking mild to you, you golfing bastard!'

And sure enough, the doc was due on the links in, like, jig time, so he didn't have a whole lot of time to mutter the platitudes. The woman was whining blue murder and he wanted to say,

'You'll get used to it.'

She never did.

Never.

When her husband heard, he did what was becoming more common: he fucked off.

Permanently.

Then the legion of social workers pitched in, with their Gestapo suggestions.

'Give him up for adoption.'

Right.

They were just lining up to grab a child with Down

syndrome. Ten grand bought them a cherubic dote from Russia or the Third World.

Tess was brief in her response to the suggestions.

'Fuck off.'

She raised Tom with every ounce of spirit and guts she had. Got him through school, then found him a job in a warehouse. Sometimes, the gods there be cut a poor bitch some slack, not much but a thread. The lads in the warehouse were all from Tess's neighbourhood, Bohermore, one of the few real communities in the city. They watched out for him. He began as a messenger boy, then, over the years, thanks to the lads, he learned to drive a forklift and that was one shit-proud day for all.

Not to mention the extra few euros it brought into their home.

Tom was tall, unusual for his condition, with dark hair, the eyes of a fawn and the nature of an angel. The day he got to drive the forklift, he literally ran home to tell his mum, shouting,

'Mum . . . Mum, I got me licence, I can drive the big machine.'

She wiped her tears away, said,

'So, takeaway curry tonight and your favourite movie.'

Die Hard Three.

If only she knew how ominous that was.

Truth to tell, Tom would watch anything with Bruce Willis in it. Tess watched him as he watched the movie, wondering if he thought he *was* Bruce Willis.

*

Their life wasn't exactly easy but they relished what they had: primarily each other.

Friday evening, Tom got his wages, and had his ritual in place. Go to Holland's shop, be polite to Mary, buy the big box of Dairy Milk for his mum and then walk home. In Holland's, a girl, looking through the postcards, smiled at him and he blushed.

He got his purchases and left. He walked along Eyre Square and headed up Prospect Hill; he always quickened his pace when he came to the alley that led to St Patrick's Church. It had shadows and he didn't like them. Then the customer from the shop, the pretty girl appeared, asked,

'Could you help me, please?'

His mum had instilled in him the virtue of always helping people. But the alley?

The girl had a lovely smile, said,

'I dropped my mobile in there and I'm afraid to look for it by my own self.'

Bruce Willis would help.

Tom entered the alley and immediately got a ferocious wallop to the back of his neck. Two young men stood over him, the girl right in front. She said,

'Chocolates. Oh, I so love sweetness.'

Tom got to his feet, dizzy but still able to stand, protested,

'Those are for me mum.'

One of the young men, with a livid fresh scar on his cheek, lashed out with his Doc Marten, smashing Tom's teeth, and the other asked,

'Oh, did that hurt?'

And delivered a ferocious kick to Tom's crotch.

Tom threw up all over the girl's boots. She said,

'Jesus wept, I just cleaned those.'

Tom was on his knees, still retching, and the girl knelt down to his level, asked,

'You wanna go home to your momma, that it?'

He muttered miserably and the girl said,

'But the chocolates, we can't waste them.'

One of the men grabbed Tom's head and forced open his mouth, the girl ripped open the cellophane, grabbed a fistful of the sweets and shoved them into his mouth. Then she produced a knife – Tom knew it as a Stanley from work – and she said,

'Little trouble digesting all of them, you greedy boy? Let me help you.'

And slit his throat in one practised movement.

The other man took the box of Dairy Milk, scattered the remains over Tom's falling body, said,

'Sweets for the sweet.'

The girl bent down, waited till Tom bled out, said as he gurgled,

'Christ, keep it down.'

Then rifled through his jacket, found his pay packet, said,

'Payday.'

They didn't glance back as they strolled from the alley.

4

'If you woke up breathing, congratulations!
You have another chance.'

Graffiti on the wall of the abbey

Tom Russell's stunning song 'Guadalupe', sung by the ethereal Gretchen Peters, from his powerful new album, was unwinding in my head as I crossed the Salmon Weir Bridge. Looked in vain to see a salmon leap.

Nope.

Into our third year of the water remaining:

contaminated,

poisoned,

lethal.

The bottled-water companies continued to rake in the cash. No recession for them. The rest of us poor bastards continued to boil the water.

Grudgingly.

A Garda car swerved into the cathedral car park. Call it instinct, I knew they weren't stopping to light candles.

A Ban Garda got out, wearing sergeant stripes.

Ridge.

Or in Irish, *Ní Iomaire*.

The uniform suited her. She looked kind of regal. Seeing

her, the late-winter sun bouncing off the gold buttons on her tunic, I felt the old pang. The deep regret that I'd been kicked off the Force. Ridge and I went back even further than Stewart and I. We weren't friends. More's the Irish pity.

Fate seemed to continually throw us together. I admired her. Not that I'd ever tell her. Her family had been scarred by alcoholism and she had an inbuilt loathing of alkies. My last case, she'd received a serious beating but appeared to be recovered. In so far as you ever get past such an event. I had a limp and a hearing aid, had had more broken bones than a nun has polished floors.

Ridge was gay but had married an Anglo-Irish landowner with the imposing name of Anthony Bradford-Hemple.

He regarded me as a peasant. Their marriage was truly one of convenience. He had clout, played golf with my nemesis, Superintendent Clancy, and played bridge with the elite of the city. He needed a mother for his teenage daughter; Ridge wanted promotion.

Deal done.

Seemed to be holding.

Sort of.

She leaned against the car, her face expressionless.

I said,

'Think you may have missed the noon Mass.'

She threw a brief glance at the church, said,

'Wouldn't hurt you to go the odd time.'

I gave her my best smile, full of bullshite and malevolence, said,

'I've just been in the abbey, lit some candles for all sinners.'

She seemed to have many replies to this but let it slide, said,

'You'll have heard about Father Malachy.'

I said,

'I've an alibi.'

Now her annoyance surfaced. She spat,

'Don't be such a thundering eejit.'

And a shadow of rage and compassion caressed her face as she said,

'And the other attack?'

'What?'

She looked at me, asked,

'You don't know?'

'Know what?'

But the temporary feeling of whatever had fled and she snapped,

'What am I? Your private source of information? Buy a bloody paper.'

To needle her, I asked,

'How is your husband?'

Leaned heavily on the last word.

She said,

'He's away on business.'

I moved to go, said,

'Give him my love. I'm on my way to see Malachy. You think he'd prefer grapes or a pack of cigs?'

She shrugged, cautioned,

'This is Garda business, stay out of it.'

I loved that, the tone of authority, the sheer con-descension. I said,

'I'm all done with priests. This is purely a Good Samaritan gig.'

She got back in the car, hurled,

'You need to call the Samaritans yourself.'

And burned rubber outta there.

Cops watch way too many cop shows.

Malachy was in Intensive Care, no visitors. I'd said I was a relative and was told a doctor would see me soon. The health service is so bollixed that that probably meant two days. I had a book so I didn't mind too much.

The new John Cheever biography, by the same writer who'd done the stunning bio of Richard Wright. The book sure captured the torment, agony, guilt and utter loneliness of the alcoholic. I didn't really need it described; I lived it every frigging day.

'Mr Taylor?'

A doctor, towering above me. Pristine white coat with all the pens in the top pocket. One, to my joy, was leaking. A nametag identified him as *Dr Ravin*. Not Irish then, but fuck, few were these days. They'd fucked off to where the money was.

He asked,

'You are a relative?'

Yeah, brothers in animosity, bonded in hatred and related by booze. I said,

'Yes, first cousins; we are very close.'

Close to murder, mostly.

He did the sympathy dance, I nodded idiotically, then he said,

'The padre . . .'

'Priest,' I snapped.

How often do you get to correct the medical profession? Yeah.

He said,

'My apologies. He has suffered severe trauma, he is in a coma and the next twenty-four hours are critical.'

'Will he die?'

He reassessed me. Then, maybe acknowledging I was in shock, soft-pedalled. He said,

'He is not a young man and, alas, he has not taken care of his body very well, so, as I said, the next day will be crucial.'

'Cigarettes,' I said.

He nodded, then asked if I had a number I could be reached at. I gave him the mobile one. We shook hands and he headed off to do doctorly stuff, or maybe, if my sense of smell was still vaguely intact, grab a sly cig.

I was preparing to leave when a tall, stern-looking priest marched up to me. They ever needed a poster boy for the clergy or the Gestapo, this guy was it. A shock of steel-grey hair, beautifully cut. I know, as I have the other kind. The cheap, bad version. His black suit was immaculate. If Armani was doing a clerical line, he'd got the best of the bunch. Shit, I mean, if the current Pope was releasing a CD wearing Gucci slippers, anything was up for grabs.

His face was deeply tanned and I finally understood what an aquiline nose meant.

His eyes matched his hair.

Steel.

He moved like an athlete, assured, confident, and I thought,

'*A player.*'

A tiny pin in his lapel, shining in its golden almost-simplicity.

Opus Dei.

Memo to myself:

'*Watch your wallet.*'

He extended his hand, said, not asked,

'Mr Jack Taylor.'

I took his hand, said,

'Yes.'

His grip was like the granite workers in Connemara. He smiled.

Fucking great teeth. I had great teeth but they weren't my own. He said,

'I'm Father Gabriel.'

Like I should know?

I asked,

'Like the Archangel?'

Too easy, but what the hell, how often do you get a Dan Brown moment? Especially when he said,

'You know your angels?'

And I countered,

'And my demons.'

The smile vanished. Just folded its tent and fucked off. He asked,

'Is there somewhere . . . less public, we might talk?'

I bit my tongue, asked,

'The confessional?'

He was seriously tiring of me, so I said,

'The River Inn, across the road, does a rather good lunch.'

I added the *rather* just to keep him off balance.

Some of the smile slithered back. He said,

'Capital.'

I mean, outside of Booker nominees, who talks like that?

He added,

'My treat.'

My cup fucking overfloweth.

A man brushed past me. I vaguely recognized him, a Down syndrome adult. I asked,

'How yah doing?'

He gave me a radiant smile, said,

'Wonderful, Mr Taylor, thank you.'

Oh, God, if I'd only known that brief encounter would feature large in what was to come. When I finally learned of the alley murder, I immediately thought of that lovely soul.

I just pray that I was as warm as he seemed to think I was.

Gabriel was meanwhile moving fast and I had to hurry to catch up. The guy was a power walker and he stopped, noticing my limp, said,

'I do apologize, Mr Taylor; I'm accustomed to speed.'

Bollix.

I said, teeth clenched,

'Tell you what, Gabe, you power on over there, grab the corner table and order up. They do great bacon and cabbage.'

Like Mr Perfect would ever eat such basic peasant food. He asked, smirk in place,

'And for you, Mr Taylor?'

'Pint and a Jay chaser. Oh, and call me Jack.'

His face ran a gamut of emotions, none of them exuding warmth. He said,

'Righty-ho, see you anon.'

Who the fuck was this guy? Who on heaven's earth spoke like that?

And he was gone.

Trailing coldness in his wake.

Whatever else I know, I knew bacon and cabbage wouldn't be his . . . forte?

And I seriously doubted he watched *True Blood*.

I stopped outside the hospital, saw Gabe already disappearing into the River Inn, and reached into my jacket for my cigs. Yeah, yeah, I know,

Smoking again.

Rationing them, OK?

I cranked up my Zippo – it had the logo 'FIFTH OF . . .' – and gulped down a lungful of Blue Superkings.

I moved over to the dismal smokers' shed. It should have a sign proclaiming: 'GIVE ME YOUR HUDDLED MASSES.'

A motley crew of:

frazzled nurses,
patients, I kid you not, trailing IVs,
stunned relatives,
and
Dr Ravin.

I know my kin. For once, I did the decent thing. I pretended not to see him. A man, my age, with a jaundiced pallor, on crutches, said,

'Hiya, Jack.'

I did the Irish gambit, when you haven't one flogging notion of who they are, said,

'Jesus! Haven't seen you in ages.'

He moved closer to me. He had the scent of death on him. I know it from familiarity. Said,

'I'm Gerry Malloy.'

I didn't ask,

'So how are you?'

He was on crutches, looked desperate.

He was fucked.

I lied,

'Great to see you, Gerry.'

He looked furtively around, then confided,

'I'm hoping to get a big claim out of this.'

I ground my cig under my boot, said,

'My fingers crossed for you.'

He licked his bottom lip, a gesture like the onset of dementia, said gleefully,

'If they cut off my right leg, I'm set for life.'

OK.

Before I could hazard,

'Good luck with that,'

he asked,

'Jack, could you spot me a twenty? You can see I'll be rolling in it, so no worries about payback.'

An arm and a leg, as they say.

Oh, sweet Jesus.

I gave him the note and as I limped away, he shouted,

'Big hug to your blessed mother.'

I waved . . . yeah.

She'd been dead five years but I had a feeling he might be able to deliver the hug in person sooner than he reckoned.

5

'A lapsed Catholic is simply one who is hedging his bets.'

Ridge

I arrived at the pub a long fifteen minutes after Gabriel. He'd found the corner table, and a lone ray of sunshine was beaming through. Did it illuminate him?

No.

Seemed to emphasize the aura of darkness around him – or maybe I just needed a frigging pint.

He was tucking into their famous homemade soup, dabbing at the corners of his mouth like a petulant nun. A lone pint of Guinness, forlorn in its solitude, sat opposite him, like a sin he'd refused to absolve. I indicated the chair across from him and he waved me to it. The waitress – a rarity, she was Irish – approached, said,

'Hiya, Jack.'

He gave me a look, like, how often are you in here?

I gave her my best smile and meant it. She turned to Gabe, asked,

'Father, have you decided on your main course?'

He had. Demanded, not asked,

'The Dover sole, lightly grilled. Are the vegetables fresh?'

'Yes, Father, we had a delivery just this morning.'

He never looked at her. This guy was accustomed to *hired help*. He said,

'I'll have the Brussels sprouts, a side salad of coleslaw, and red onions – in olive-oil dressing, of course.'

She risked a glance at me, her eyes saying,

'*Bollix*.'

She asked,

'Usual, Jack?'

'That would be great, thanks.'

He looked up, queried,

'You eat here regularly?'

'Drink. I drink here . . . regularly.'

Like this was news to him.

He reached down, picked up a beautiful brown-leather briefcase with a symbol on it:

T.

B.

E.

I thought I knew it, but couldn't bring it to mind then.

I would later, ruefully . . . as I learned it meant 'The Brethren, Eternally.'

I said,

'You didn't have that in the hospital.'

He was mildly impressed, said,

'A keen observer, that's good, very good. My driver brought it over.'

He had a driver? I asked,

'DUI, that it?'

The briefcase was snapped open – and I mean *snapped* –
then shut again. Then he rested his tanned hands on it and,
fuck, were his nails . . . manicured?

His tone was now that of a stern parent to an unruly
child. He said,

'I know all about your smart mouth, your – how shall I
put it? – *cynical repartee*, but it's wasted on me, so let's drop
the smart-alec pose, shall we?'

I threw him with a nonchalant,

'Fine.'

His chastisements obviously carried huge weight in his
usual circles. He asked,

'I beg your pardon?'

'Isn't Jesus about love, spreading the joy, or are you more
of the school that *'Man is born of woman and is full of
misery'*?

He leaned back, folded those perfect hands in his lap,
said,

'You remember your Catechism.'

'No, I remember me funerals.'

His food came. He snapped at the girl,

'Glass of sparkling water, very thin wedge of lemon.'

Waved her away.

I said,

'*Bon appétit.*'

I hoped it choked him. He didn't answer, set about his
food like a rabid dog, ate with a ferocious determination.

This was his food and by Christ he was going to have every last bite. I drank, thanked the girl when she brought my Jameson, and waited for whatever this prick had in mind.

Finished, he cleaned the corners of his mouth delicately with the napkin, took a sip of water, said,

'To business.'

'I can hardly contain myself.'

The briefcase snapped open again. He took a fat envelope, passed it over to me, said,

'A retainer.'

I didn't touch it. He stared straight into my eyes. I knew he didn't much care for what he saw there. He said,

'The Church, as you are well aware, has been under intense scrutiny; the errors of the few have cast a shadow on the many.'

I nearly laughed out loud.

Fucking *errors*!

Echoed,

'You mean

the child molesters,

the Magdalen girls,

our local bishop, who refuses to resign despite the whole country howling for his head?'

He winced.

An actual physical tic appeared under his left eye, began a rat-tat-tat like the drumbeat of the fallen.

He reined it in, said,

'Recovery must come from within. To that end, a group

58

was formed within the Church to deal with misconduct before it becomes public.'

I said,

'A splinter group, like the Provos breaking from the official IRA?'

His efforts to control his temper were admirable. He almost sneered,

'I don't believe we have been accused of bearing arms?'

I said,

'Yet.'

And before he could respond, I added,

'Least with the IRA, we could see the weapons.'

He asked, in a patient, icy tone,

'Might I continue?'

'Go for it, Gabe.'

'Our reform group are known as the Brethren, and, despite your cynicism, Mr Taylor, we have managed to avoid further unsavoury revelations.'

He said *avoid*. I heard *cover up*. I let him drone on.

'Alas, our chief fundraiser and most active member, Father Loyola Dunne, seems to have disappeared.'

I sat back, let the moment linger, then said,

'Let me guess: him and your slush fund?'

He was silent, seething.

I pushed,

'How much?'

He had to drag it from deep down, said through gritted teeth,

'Three quarters of a million.'

I gave an appreciative whistle, said,

'And you can't go the official route. You want him found *discreetly*. No, let me rephrase that: you want the cash back?'

His eyes burned on me.

'In a nutshell, yes.'

I said,

'Tried Vegas?'

His patience with me was well gone. He shook his head, slipped a hand in the briefcase, slid over a photograph, said,

'This is Loyola; his details are on the back.'

A man in his late fifties, with a kind face, laughter lines on the eyes, high forehead, but deep bags under his eyes, heavy jowled.

I asked,

'A drinker?'

Tight smile, then,

'None of us is without our frailties.'

'Want to share some of yours, Gabe, help us . . . bond?'

He shut down. The meeting was over. He handed me a tiny white card, with three phone numbers, said,

'You report only to me, and need I stress that speed is of the essence?'

I nearly gave the Nazi salute, but too obvious. I flicked his card on to the table, said,

'You're forgetting the important bit.'

Finally, with a look of surprise, he indicated the fat envelope, said,

'I think you'll find the fee more than generous, and

a speedy resolution will result in a very handsome bonus.'

I said,

'You don't listen too good, do you, Gabe? So I'll say it slow, you might be able to hear it then. I haven't said I'll take the job.'

His lips literally peeled back to reveal those marvellous teeth. He said,

'Mr Taylor, you are a Catholic – lapsed, perhaps, but still part of our flock. You have helped the Church in the past, albeit reluctantly, I understand, but surely you want to see the Church restored to its former glory?'

Restored to its bullying days, its arrogance, its total disregard of the people. I had an overwhelming desire to wallop him with a powerful right hand on his tanned face, wipe out one or two of those perfect teeth.

I said,

'I'll take the case. One, because I think you're lying through your teeth. Two, it's a blast to be actually receiving money from the Church. But know this, Gabe, I don't *report* and I'm not – no way – part of your flock, lapsed or otherwise.'

It was impossible to gauge how he took it. He stood, said,

'I have covered our dinner bill.'

I asked,

'When was Loyola last seen?'

He was already leaving, said,

'He gave the eleven o'clock Mass in his parish ten days ago and then disappeared.'

He strode off, master of all he surveyed. A vague rumour

of piety in his wake. He hadn't wished me 'God bless.'

In lieu, I counted the cash, a blessing in its commercial self.

Later I picked up some books from Charlie Byrne's bookshop. Vinny, in full metal, said,

'They're preparing a flood fund for the families devastated by the rains.'

I said,

'Why don't they just use their usual slush fund?'

I bought a shitload of books, including:

Jason Starr,

Craig McDonald,

Tom Piccirilli,

R. J. Ellory,

Megan Abbott.

Vinny said,

'Nice selection.'

I also picked up Carol O'Connell. I don't care what anyone says, Mallory was a definite influence on Stieg Larsson.

In *Find Me*, there's a passage that scalds my soul.

He asked her,

'Why don't you want to have kids?'

Mallory said,

'Because I don't know what they're for.'

My apartment in Nun's Island was sublet to me by a guy who decided to take a gap year in his late forties. Some gap. Reeked more of a mid-life crisis, but better, I guess, than a red sports car. He showed no inclination to return and I wasn't encouraging him. Nun's Island is a small neighbourhood, nestling close to the cathedral.

And, yes, there are nuns.

The Poor Clares.

An enclosed community. Simply to enter their grounds was to find a rare tranquillity. To tread lightly on holy ground. They were currently running a campaign to pay for the restoration of the convent. Titled 'Buy a Brick'.

You bought a brick by buying a ticket which then went forward to a lotto. Being newly flush with cash, I went to them, offered the Mother Superior fifty euros. She protested it was too much. She noticed me staring at her neck. Nuns, like cops, see everything. I thought, *'If you're staring at a nun's neck, you need a brick.'*

Hard, to the side of your head.

I was entranced by the necklace she wore. It appeared to be tiny beautiful stones, threaded through a silver chain. Each stone had a letter. She was delighted I'd noticed, said,

'It reads "Medjugorje".'

I asked,

'You've been?'

She shook her head at such an idea, said,

'No, my sister went, and, you know, she said the sun danced in the sky.'

Like all nuns, she had that flawless skin. Why the cosmetic companies aren't researching them is a mystery. Her eyes were clear blue, lit with a lovely hint of devilment. She asked,

'What do you think of that?'

I had no idea, said,

'I've no idea.'

She pulled out a batch of cards, asked,

'Your name, please, for the draw?'

'It's Jack, but honest to God, no need to put me on the tickets.'

She seemed surprised, so I tried,

'I've never been lucky.'

I was about to leave when she took the piece from round her neck and slipped it over my head. I began,

'I can't—'

She said,

'Better be blessed than lucky.'

That moved me so.

Go figure.

My last encounter with a nun had resulted in murder. Outside, the sky was darkening and the deadly ice they were predicting seemed to hang, waiting. A guy was selling DVDs. I guess he figured even nuns watched movies.

Newly blessed, I bought:

Orphan,

Traitor,

Passengers,

District 9,

And, I swear to God, Sam Raimi's

Drag Me to Hell.

There is some mega-metaphysical irony in all the above, but I'm fucked if I can join the dots.

As I headed off, the guy said,

'Cool chain, dude; Medjugorje rocks.'

Bono must have played there.

A new off-licence had opened, the budget had been announced and . . . the price of booze had been lowered. In a country decimated by alcohol, they were encouraging us to drink. It had state-of-the-art premises and even offered loyalty cards! And brews you'd never see ordinarily, so I stocked up on my favourite hard-to-get brands:

Shiner Bock,

Blue Moon,

Asahi,

Sam Adams.

I'm an alkie, I'm hurting, I'll drink anything, even after-shave, and have done so.

Though I suggest you avoid Old Spice.

But as Derek Raymond said in *The Crust on its Uppers*, I can be a beer buff.

What this flashy new place showed was, though we were deep in recession, we were not only drinking as mad as ever, but with some discernible taste.

I got back to my apartment, anticipating a blast of 'Blue Moon' and twenty minutes of Johnny Duhan's new album.

I had a wad of cash in my jacket, new DVDs, the literal blessing of a good nun and a new case. And Laura would soon be coming from London.

How good can it get?

I don't do happy.

But I was real close then.

Wouldn't I just love to be the poster boy for Prozac, have a kick-arse smile perpetually in place, plaster my face on those Prozac bottles with the logo 'WE REST OUR CASE.'

But my past was too littered with the wasted and the wounded.

Ever hear Marc Roberts sing 'Dust In The Storm'? Listen and weep.

I'm not a total eejit, I'll grab the moments of peace, fleeting though they be, when they deign to appear. That's how I was feeling.

Opened the door of the apartment to a ton of junk.

I'd won 10 million in the Nigerian Lottery, got a voucher for a free pizza from Papa Joe's, an appeal for orphans. Then I came to a small, tightly wrapped parcel.

In black paper.

Uh-oh.

Neatly printed in red Gothic lettering on the front was,

'Jack Taylor.'

Not good. A gut feeling. I fingered the Medjugorje chain round my neck.

My apartment opens up to a large room, which has the books, TV and laptop, and leads to a small kitchen. A marble-top counter from Connemara constitutes the dining area. I placed the package there and pulled back from it. Opened the fridge, pulled out a Shiner, drained half that in jig time. No shite, but those Texans make good beer. I approached the package as if it were incendiary. My history of such mail was all bad.

Took a deep breath and tore it open.

Out on to the marble top fell a perfect miniature sculpture.

A headstone,

the size of a Zippo.

I stared at it, muttering,

'The fuck is this?'

It was exquisitely carved, polished to a high sheen.

In any other circumstances, I'd have admired the sheer artistry. In a state of alert, I reached for the dictionary, looked up the definition for 'headstone', got 'a stone at the head of a grave'.

All my instincts screaming,

'Throw it out . . . NOW!'

No coincidence that the clocks were due to go back to winter time, and when that happened, it was a long time to the light. If the package was meant to unnerve me, it did.

I felt the urge to get the hell out of there, be among people. Put on my all-weather Garda coat and slip in the side pocket the Walther PPK I'd had since the time of the Devil. Just the weight of it eased my growing paranoia.

Once outside, I felt better – not great, but getting there. What I needed was a large Jameson, but maybe some caffeine would be wiser first.

I turned left at Nun's Island, moved along to the low bridge close to the Samaritans, stole a furtive glance at Mill

Street, the Garda headquarters, with a pang.

'*Never to belong there no more.*'

Muttered,

'Get a grip.'

Turned left again and across O'Brien's bridge. St Patrick's school loomed large and off-white. In my time, the teachers were mostly Patrician Brothers. They wore a green sash like a belt and were very fond of the reed cane. They could lash with impunity and did. At least once a week, I'd stagger home, my legs bruised and battered, welts clearly visible on the bare skin. No one questioned their authority. They walloped the be-jaysus out of you, it was simply the norm.

It wasn't that they were always right, simply that a cowed populace never thought to ask if they might be wrong.

All has changed, utterly. Corporal punishment is illegal. And in a ferocious, ironic turnaround, the teachers are now the ones being bullied.

I had replaced their reeds of punishment with a whole new way of lacerating myself.

Called it Jameson.

Stood there for a moment, thinking.

If I continued to dig the hole, I was going to need the headstone sooner than expected.

6

'Always do sober what you said you'd do drunk.
That will keep your mouth shut.'

Irish proverb

I walked down Quay Street, stepped into Café du Journal. Real Irish place, right?

I half hoped I'd run into Vinny from Charlie Byrne's bookshop, but, no, the place was half empty. I got a corner table – old cop habit, so you can see who's coming at you. Ordered a double espresso and a large Danish. I had no appetite, but figured it would soak up the inevitable Jay. The sugar rush wouldn't hurt either. Far end of the café was a Goth girl. I've always had a soft spot for them. They are harmless, do their gig, despite ridicule, and carry a continuous torch for The Cure.

I admire tenacity.

The girl, beneath the white make-up, black eyeshadow, black lipstick, couldn't have been more than nineteen. She was staring right back at me. She was pretty, in a sort of wounded way; even the Goth stuff couldn't quite hide that. Her eyes, a deep brown, were literally boring into mine, so I asked,

'Help you with something?'

She moved from her table and took the seat opposite me. When she spoke, I noticed the stud in her tongue. How do they eat with that?

Maybe they don't.

She said,

'You don't know me.'

Statement.

I asked,

'Any reason why I should?'

Allowing a hint of force in there. If she was here to bust my balls, she'd chosen the right fucking day and the right fucking time to try it.

Her accent was the new cultivated Irish that spoke of:

money,

education,

confidence,

and fuck you.

As alien to me as a Brit.

She said,

'You put my brother in the mental hospital.'

As lines go, it's a showstopper.

'What?'

She took my spoon, asked,

'May I?'

Cut a corner off my Danish, said,

'I like sweet things.'

She'd thrown me. The only person I knew for sure I'd put in the home for the bewildered was my own self. Then,

Jesus Christ.

Years ago, a young man had been beheading swans. I'd nailed him and, yeah, he came from a *good* family, meaning cash and clout. No jail time, sent to a hospital. She asked,

'Coming back, dude? The booze hasn't destroyed all the brain cells?'

I'd met most brands of psychos during my career as a half-arsed investigator. They all shared the same total lack of empathy. Not so much that they lacked a human element, more like they were a whole other species. A highly lethal one. But that kid, he'd used a Samurai sword to decapitate the swans. What I most recalled was the absolute glee in his eyes. He didn't so much enjoy his deeds as revel in them. I'd used a stun gun to knock him back in the water. The swans had gone for his eyes. He lost one. Every fibre of my being had wanted to let him drown. But I'd dragged him out. I'd hoped never to see the creep again.

Years later, he'd turned up.

'*Cured*,' he told me.

The medicine hadn't been invented to rewire his kind. They simply changed their act. The deadly impulse was even more honed and ferocious than ever. He'd then vanished from my radar. I always knew he was out there and I was 'unfinished business'.

I said,

'I remember him; he told me he was a student.'

She gave me a look of pure defiance, said,

'He got his degree.'

I couldn't resist, said,

'Long as it wasn't as a vet.'

She pushed the Danish back, said,

'It's stale.'

'So . . . ?'

'He's missing.'

I wanted to say, '*He was born missing*,' but went with,

'And I should care . . . why?'

'I want you to find him.'

I laughed, said,

'I'm the very last person he'd want on his case. You never gave me your name.'

Her whole body language was screaming that she had ammunition. She said,

'Bethany.'

I signalled to the waitress for the bill, said,

'Your family, as I recall, has lots of resources, and at the last count there were nine professional investigators in the city. They'd be glad to take your money. Me, I couldn't give a rat's arse what happens to your whacko brother.'

I paid the bill, stood up, and was turning to leave when she near whispered,

'I have something you want, Taylor.'

I shook my head, had already reached the door when she hissed,

'I know what happened to the priest.'

Pause.

'And the retard.'

That stopped me. But she was up and brushing past me, moving fast. I went after her.

Great. Pursuing a young girl on the busiest street in Galway.

My mobile shrilled, I said,

'Fuck.'

Pulled it from my jacket. Bethany had reached McDonagh's fish 'n' chip shop at the bottom of Quay Street. Christ, that girl could move. She turned, stared back at me, then ever so elegantly gave me the finger. She disappeared among the hordes of tourists being offloaded from a coach.

I answered the mobile.

'Jack, it's Stewart.'

'Yeah?'

'Where are you?'

'Iraq.'

'What?'

'The bottom of Quay Street. The fuck does it matter where I am?'

He wasn't fazed, he'd heard it too often. Said,

'I'm at the Meyrick, can you come? We need to talk.'

I said, 'OK,' and rang off. The Meyrick used to be the Great Southern Hotel. It was never 'Great' but it was one more fading landmark on the city's landscape. I've always had a sneaking fondness for it, mainly as they allow me in. It had moved further up the ladder in its new incarnation. And me, I just got older.

I headed up Shop Street, marvelling at the new outlets, a new one every day. The street was ablaze with buskers, mimes, panhandlers, and the dying remnants of a drinking school. I stopped outside the GBC café. The name had come to me. Bethany's brother broke the surface of my bedraggled mind.

Ronan Wall.

The last time I'd met him, he'd been charm personified. You'd think he'd have had a hard-on for me. But no, despite his eye loss, his incarceration in the mental hospital, you'd swear I was his best friend. Did he, as you'd expect, lacerate me, berate me for destroying his life?

Nope.

He thanked me!

I shit thee not.

Said, and I quote,

'Thanks to you, Jack Taylor, I've turned my life around. I have great plans for my future.'

My arse.

He was the real McCoy, a full-blown psycho, the out-and-out ultimate predator, and he'd learned to hide in plain sight. He could mimic human behaviour to a degree of charm that probably fooled most people. A good-looking kid, blond hair falling into his remaining eye. The new artificial one was, no doubt, the best money could buy, but disconcerting in its stillness. His good eye couldn't quite disguise what lay beneath and, worse, he knew I knew.

But he'd rattled on, flush with affability and studied warmth.

I hadn't seen him since, but I knew one day he'd show, and so here he was again in my life. Whatever the gig, it wouldn't be good. How could it, with a stone killer just biding his time?

*

The Meyrick Hotel lies at the bottom of Eyre Square and the new renovations should have made it imposing. All that solid granite, the iron railings, but to me it was still the hotel of my youth. I pushed through the freshly polished glass door, saw Stewart in the lounge. A white porcelain teapot and matching cups before him. Decaffeinated or herbal tea, no doubt. He stood up on seeing me. Dressed in an Armani suit, one of those suits that whispered to you,

'*You ain't never going to be able to afford this.*'

He was the personification of the new Irish: sleek, smug self-containment. I felt like his bedraggled grandfather. We sat, he offered me some of the shite stuff he was drinking, and I gave him the look. Asked,

'What's up?'

He reached in the pocket of the immaculate suit, produced a small package, said,

'This came in the post.'

I said,

'A headstone.'

His surprise was evident, so I said,

'I got one too.'

He glanced at the package, said,

'It's unnerving.'

I gave a short laugh.

'That's the point.'

He waited, apparently believing I had an answer.

I didn't. Finally, he tried,

'Would it be some kind of Hallowe'en prank?'

I said,

'Trick or Threat?'

I told him about Ronan Wall's sister and her parting shot about Father Malachy. Stewart was edgy. He liked patterns, things that made sense, events he could Zen control. His mobile shrilled and he checked the screen, said,

'I have to take this, Jack.'

Like I gave a fuck?

While he talked, I played with ordering a large Jay, decided the distaste on Stewart's face wasn't worth the hassle. He finished the call, said,

'Sorry about that – a new venture.'

He'd been a dope-dealer, got busted, did a long jail stretch, and since then I knew he'd been involved in all sorts of business gigs. He never shared details but was always awash with cash. For once, I asked,

'What is it?'

He grimaced, said,

'You're going to laugh.'

'I could do with a decent laugh.'

He flexed his fingers, then said,

'Head shops.'

He was right, I laughed. Galway already had two of them, selling:

> herbal joints,
> bongs,
> high Es,
> flying angels,
> rockets,
> chill.

And all the assorted paraphernalia of a doper. A crazy legal loophole allowed all sorts of legal highs to be purchased. How fitting that a convicted ex-dealer would get a slice of the action. I shook my head and he asked,
'You disapprove?'
I stood up, said,
'No, I think it's brilliant.'
He came as close to a plea as his nature allowed, asked,
'What about the headstone?'
I thought,
'Headstone . . . head shop.'
Said,
'You'll make a killing.'

7

'The old people believe a headstone is your last word.'

Jack's dad

Putting headstones out of my mind, I figured I'd better begin my search for the rogue priest.

Where would a renegade cleric with stolen money go?

As far as possible.

But maybe not.

Back to basics: use my feet. I trudged the town, showing his photo. It's a given: you do this kind of tedious work, you're on a hiding to nothing. People will give you answers. It's Ireland, no one is ever . . . ever, going to simply say,

'No.'

Would that they could, but they can't.

Mostly they asked,

'Why?'

'What's he done?'

'What's in it for me?'

And of course, lots of misinformation. You had to follow that shite anyway.

Mostly what you got was tired. My limp ached. I even did a Google search. Nope. He had really flown under the radar.

Eventually, I had to phone Gabriel, give him my report. A very short one. I played with the idea of stringing him along, saying I had a definite lead. When I called him, his clipped sarcastic tone changed that idea.

Quick.

I hoped he'd fire me. I never wanted to have to listen to this sanctimonious gob-shite again.

I'd begun the call with,

'It's Jack Taylor.'

He snapped,

'I know that.'

Great start. I tried,

'I've been tracking down every avenue of investigation.'

'And?'

Jesus, I disliked this bollix, said,

'And . . .'

Let it hang for max impact, then,

'. . . I got nothing.'

Silence – an ominous one.

Then he ordered,

'Stay on it.'

Notice the lack of *please*? I fucking did, said,

'What?'

'Are you deaf, Taylor?'

Well actually, yes, in one ear, but I didn't feel this was the time to share.

He continued in a curt, no-shite tone,

'I'll expect more positive news in your next report.'

Report!

I said,

'Your money, pal.'

He near shouted,

'Not *my* money, the Lord's!'

Is there a reply to this kind of spiritual mugging? He ended with,

'You'd be wise to remember, Taylor, that God is watching.'

'A divine accountant, no less.'

Rang off and thought,

'*Pray that.*'

You want to find a priest, there is one, dare I say, infallible route.

Ask a nun.

I knew exactly my pigeon. My previous case, I'd met a Sister Maeve. Like most of my relationships, it began well. Then, per rote, came apart. I liked her a lot, but she, like so many others, had come to despise me. I'd say loathe, but I'm not sure nuns have that one in their training manual.

She taught at the mercy school in Newtownsmith, beside the Electricity Board. What the ESB failed to electrify, the teenage girls made up for. The name of the school in Irish has a lovely resonance:

'*Scoil An Leanbh Íosa.*'

Last time I'd met her, a huge construction site was in full roar opposite. Now complete, it was a mega retail outlet, named, I shit thee not . . . Born. I walked down there, stopped at Holland's shop, got a warm hello from

Mary, God bless her, bought a large box of Dairy Milk.

Beware of gimps bearing gifts.

I glanced at the tabloids, all ablaze with the tragic suicide of the German goalkeeper. I said a silent Hail Mary for him.

Sé do bheatha, a Mhuire . . .

Passed down by the Town Hall, advertising the coming appearance of Steve Earle. I loved his singing and, even more, his role in *The Wire*. 'Galway Girl' began to unreel in my head.

At the school reception, I asked if I might have a moment with Sister Maeve.

'Yes.'

Was she glad to see me?

Take a wild fucking guess.

She had aged, but then, apart from Donny Osmond, who hadn't? She fixed me with those clear, unyielding blue eyes, said,

'Mr Taylor.'

In nun speak,

'*Aw fuck, not you.*'

I said,

'Jack . . . please.'

Her eyes gave away the disdain the name deserved. Establishing from the get-go, *You are no friend of mine*. Yet, during our brief time before, there had been genuine affection building. The death of a former nun had banjaxed that. I offered the chocolates, she said,

'No, thank you.'

86

I felt whipped.

I asked,

'If I might have five minutes of your time?'

Before, we'd gone for coffee. I remembered her child-like joy in a slice of Danish, coupled with a frothy cappuccino. She said,

'We'll step into the recreation room.'

We did.

She indicated we sit at a hard wooden table. Seemed appropriate. She folded her hands, asked,

'How may I assist you, Mr Taylor?'

I tried to ease the level of frigidity present, inquired,

'How have you been, Sister?'

'The Lord provides.'

Jesus wept, the usual wall of spiritual gobbledy-gook. I abandoned the ingratiation, went with,

'I've been employed by the Church.'

Paused.

Let that nugget hover.

Continued.

'To find a Father Loyola.'

The name hit.

She almost recoiled, actually moving physically from the table, as if to distance herself. Deception was not in her DNA, so I pushed,

'You know him, I guess?'

She nodded, guarded.

I went for the kill.

'Do you know where I can find him?'

Long silence. I didn't try to fill it, then she said,

'He belonged to the Brethren.'

Past tense?

She knew.

I waited.

Taking a deep breath, she said,

'I imagine your employer is not so much the Church as Father Gabriel.'

The way she said his name implied she was not a fan.

I asked,

'Are they not the same?'

She gave me a look not quite of disdain but in the neighbourhood, said,

'Father Gabriel is more interested in ... *power* than piety.'

Bitterness leaked over the last words.

She fingered her rosary beads, continued,

'The Brethren started as a wonderful idea. To reform the Church from within. A return to the teaching of Our Lord, Jesus, and the hope of restoring the people's trust in their Church.'

I nearly laughed.

The sheer fucking naivety of this. Every day, the papers screamed about how the bishops continued to hide and minimize the abuse. To such an extent that the Guards were considering prosecuting them. And still, the hierarchy, entrenched in arrogance, refused to cooperate. I wanted to roar,

'*Good luck with that.*'

Went with,

'Didn't work, huh?'

She sidestepped my sarcasm, said,

'In the beginning, it did so well. Later it emerged that Father Gabriel had another agenda. A return to the fundamentalism that would bring the people to their knees. Father Loyola believed that if he removed their funding, they'd be powerless.'

I said,

'Gabriel sounds like an ecclesiastical hit squad.'

She nearly smiled, said,

'That is bordering on sarcasm, Mr Taylor, but Father Gabriel is not a man to be crossed. They even have a motto: The Brethren, Eternally.'

The initials on his sharp briefcase.

They were sounding like the militant wing of Dominus Deo.

Cut-to-the-chase time. I asked,

'Do you know where I can find him?'

If she told me, my case would be wrapped right there. I could wipe the smug look off Gabriel's face, pocket my fee, and look forward to Laura's imminent arrival.

She was on the verge of answering when her whole body shuddered. I recognized the effect. In Ireland it's called 'When someone walks on your grave.'

She stared at me and, oh sweet Jesus, I saw fear and terror in her eyes.

She said, as if she was channelling something,

'You have recently been in a dark place.'

Recently!

Like the last twenty years of my banjaxed life.

But she was right. I'd met the Devil, up close and way too personal.

I said,

'It's true. I got to glimpse into the very mouth of hell.'

Tad dramatic, but close to the truth.

She shook her head, nigh screamed,

'No . . . no, Mr Taylor, you have it wrong, Hell looked into you.'

For fuck's sake.

I tried again.

'Will you tell me where Father Loyola is?'

She was in some kind of trance. When she did speak, it was in a flat dull monotone.

'The rains are coming; it will rain for nigh forty days and nights.'

Welcome to Galway.

Then she stood, literally shook herself, and fled from the room.

I sat for a moment, the box of chocolates like a severe reprimand, muttered,

'Great. Scaring the be-jaysus out of a nun.'

I got to me feet, trying to make sense of her words. Whatever else, she sure as shooting was right about the weather. Outside, I looked at the skies, dull grey and with the tinge of darkness that speaks of worse to come. A wino was perched on the small wall close to the Salmon Weir Bridge. I thought,

'*Precarious the pose.*'

He stared at me with bloodshot hopeless eyes, asked,

'Got anything?'

I gave him the chocolates. He snarled, muttered, 'Fucking chocolate,' and tossed the box in the river. Asked,

'Got anything else?'

I gave him twenty euros and said,

'Some advice.'

He grasped the money in a dirty fist, looked up, asked,

'And what's the freaking advice?'

I was already moving on, said,

'Steal a raincoat.'

8

'A win doesn't feel as good as a loss feels bad.'

Andre Agassi, from his memoir *Open*

And true indeed, it rained for nigh on forty days.

Downright biblical.

But despite flood devastation, the tabloids continued feeding on Tiger Woods. The fallout being that a nine iron was becoming the weapon of choice. The Guards had issued a strike notice, creating a fascinating conundrum: if it was illegal for them to strike, who was going to arrest them?

The army?

The nurses were again threatening industrial action. Sean O'Casey, our finest playwright, had written nearly ninety years ago,

'Th' whole worl's in a terrible state o' chassis.'

i.e., fucked.

I had a priest to find. He'd been parish priest at the small church in Bohermore where I made my First Communion. It was my last resort. I stopped in at Richardson's pub, holding point at the right wing of Eyre Square. It was that rarity, a family pub.

Got a stool at the counter, ordered a pint.

Ireland had recently introduced the Pour Your Own. The deal being, you were given a meter that clocked every time you poured your own. At the evening's end, you paid your bill.

Sweet fuck, was nothing sacred?

The whole buzz of a pub was watching a competent barman take his sweet time nourishing your pint and creaming off the head. If I wanted to pour my own, I'd stay home.

The pint came, splendid in all its black music. John, the barman, said,

'Haven't seen you for a bit, Jack.'

This was a subtle lash, meaning,

'You've been taking your business elsewhere, yah bollix.'

I was saved from a lame defence by a customer who said,

'Liam Clancy is dead.'

The end of an era indeed. Bob Dylan had called The Clancy Brothers the finest ballad singers ever.

What the fuck was he smoking back then?

Still, I raised my glass, said,

'Codladh sámh dó.'

Safe sleep.

I asked John,

'You ever see Father Loyola?'

His church was less than a brief rosary away. John gave a warm smile, said,

'Oh yeah, he'd stop in for a small Paddy once a week.'

In the current climate, that could be hugely misconstrued. John meant Paddy's, regarded by many as the true Irish whiskey. Above John's head was a massive flatscreen TV.

The top story was whether a children's toy was safe. Literally as a footnote, the irritating bottom-line script announced that the hundredth British soldier had been killed in Afghanistan. I pulled myself back to John, ran a scam, asked,

'He sure relied on that housekeeper of his.'

Did he have one? The fuck I knew. But some things thankfully don't change. He said,

'Ah, Maura, the poor creature, the salt of the earth, she loves her port, but she's been devastated since he left.'

Gotcha.

You don't tip Irish barmen.

I do.

And did.

John nodded, said,

'Much appreciated, Jack.'

I headed for St Patrick's church, stopping at a new off-licence to buy a bottle of port. My mobile shrilled.

Stewart.

He said Father Malachy was still in a coma. I ran the encounter with Ronan Wall's sister by him. He said,

'The swan-killer. You caught him, yeah?'

Added,

'You were a local hero for a while.'

I said,

'It didn't last.'

He countered with,

'Jack, with you, what does?'

I bit down on my temper, said,

'I think the headstone, Ronan Wall and his sister are somehow all connected.'

'Why?'

'The fuck do I know why? Call it a former hero's hunch.'

I knew he was laughing. He said,

'Lemme guess, you want me to track down the sister, and maybe even the bold Ronan himself?'

I counted to ten, said,

'What do you think I pay you for?'

Feigning indignation, he said,

'You've never paid me a single euro.'

Now I nearly smiled, said,

'Money is not the only currency. Zen that.'

And clicked off.

The priest's house was a neat bungalow to the side of the new church. The bungalow had been freshly painted and looked welcoming. Maybe he'd spent the stolen cash on that.

I knocked on the door. It was opened by a tiny robust woman, late sixties with her grey hair scraped back in a severe bun. How do women do that, and, more importantly, why?

I literally rushed her.

'Maura, just great to see you!'

Offered the port in the same frenzied tone.

She was taken aback, but I was already inside and I knew

she wasn't sure how the hell that had happened. I upped the bullshite.

'You look great, alanna.'

Paused to let the flattery sink in, then pressed on.

'I'm so sorry it's been a while, but I promised Loyola I'd call the minute I got back.'

Still perplexed, she led me into the sitting room. A massive portrait of the Sacred Heart was perched above a roaring turf fire. Is there a finer sight? I saw some framed photos of a benign smiling priest, thought,

'*I'll be having me one of those.*'

I said,

'God, I'm perished.'

Meaning . . . frozen.

She took the hint and went to make hot ports. I followed her into the kitchen. It was spotless and I startled her all over again.

Good.

I wanted her to be on the precipice continuously.

I said,

'In you go and sit by the fire, I'll make the hot port.'

She left reluctantly, her look saying,

'*Should I call the Guards now, or call after the port?*'

The port won.

The kettle boiled and I added lethal amounts of port to her mug, then pulled out the Jameson from me other pocket and added a serious dollop to hers and just the Jay for me own self.

Found the sugar, ladled three spoons into hers. Brought out the two mugs.

She was sitting on the edge of the armchair, ready to flee.
I handed her the mug, said,

'Loyola loved a wee drop of port.'

Toasted,

'*Sláinte.*'

And she took a homicidal swallow of the drink. Her eyes
danced in her head.

'I'm so sorry, I probably shouldn't have overdone the
sugar.'

She gasped,

'Oh no, 'tis lovely.'

She took another large dose and I could see it relax her. I
said,

'Ah, Loyola, those were the days, and when I entered the
Guards and he the Seminary, we still stayed in touch.'

She managed,

'You're a Guard?'

She was unwinding. I said,

'Retired now, but I do miss it.'

The latter being the only truth I told.

I asked,

'So where is the bold man himself?'

Her eyes kept flicking to a small framed photo that was
near hidden behind the host of other frames. I rattled on
about the great times we'd had fishing and other nonsense.
Finishing her drink, she asked,

'Another?'

'Lovely.'

Soon as she headed for the kitchen, a barely noticeable

stagger in her walk, I was up and grabbed the frame, put it in my pocket.

On returning, she said,

'I left out the sugar, is that all right?'

I nodded, asked,

'So where do I find my old friend?'

She looked to her left, i.e. *lying.* I'd watched Series One of *Lie to Me.*

She said, slowly, doing that careful dance round words you know are trying to be slurred,

'He's away on parish business.'

I acted irritated, pulled my phone from my pocket, looked at the screen, said,

'Please excuse me, Maura, I'll have to take this.'

That she hadn't heard the ring tone was overridden by the booze.

I said to the silent phone,

'What? Now?'

I nearly believed there was someone at the other end, acted like I'd rung off, said,

'Emergency at home. I'll have to run, I'm afraid.'

I was up and leaving. The drink had her rooted to the chair, she tried to rise, failed.

I said,

'I'll be back next week and we can have a proper chat.'

And I was outta there.

9

'We must get into step, a lockstep towards the prison of death. There is no escape. The weather will not change.'

Henry Miller, *Tropic of Cancer*

Ridge knew her marriage was over. As a gay woman, she'd married Anthony because of who he was.

He had serious clout. Played golf with the people who ran the city. Anthony simply wanted a mother for his teenage daughter and a lady of the manor for functions. Sex just wasn't in the picture. Ridge looked good, knew how to behave, and he believed he could mould her into some semblance of aristocracy, like breaking in a horse.

Before the marriage, Ridge had lived in a small house at the bottom of Devon Park. On a quiet day, you could almost hear the ocean. It was an oasis of gentility between Salthill and the city. She loved that house and just couldn't bear to sell it. She rented it to an ex-lover named Jenny. More and more, she was drawn back to her old life, to intimacy and some remnants of integrity.

Two years ago, as a favour to Jack, she'd gone on a routine call. Some girls were bullying a Down syndrome child and she'd intended to give a quiet caution to the girls in this family. Neither she nor Jack realized their father was an up-and-coming thug. He'd beaten Ridge senseless, put her in hospital.

The mastectomy she'd undergone a year before worsened her condition. She'd heard that Jack had gone after the thug in his own inimitable fashion and, for once, she was glad. Her recovery was slow and painful. She resolved never to be defenceless again. The hypocrisy of her life had begun in earnest then. Jack's treatment of the thug was never legal, she knew that. She never openly acknowledged it. She was still a Guard and Jack persisted with his philosophy of the law being for courtrooms and justice being for alleyways.

Her marriage had paid dividends. She was almost . . . almost . . . ashamed to get the rank of sergeant. Torn asunder by that incident and the coldness of her marriage, she had begun to drive to Devon Park three times a week and park outside her old house. Same time, those three days. Jack had always warned: never set up a routine; makes you a target. When her shift finished, it was as if her car headed for Devon Park. With a deep longing, she imagined Jenny curled up on the sofa, dressed in her old tracksuit, eating chicken curry and watching re-runs of *The L Word*.

Her visits became so regular, she began to notice the neighbours. Two men in their late sixties – bang on nine, they'd walk their dogs, head for the Bal, have one pint and stroll back. There was something very comforting in the regularity of their habit.

When the floods came, Ridge, like all the public sectors, was stretched to the limit. One Tuesday, after a day of ferocious depression, dealing with people who'd lost everything, she just could not face Anthony, who'd ask, without the slightest interest,

'How was work, dear?'

And before she could spill all the pain and distress, he'd add,

'A dry sherry perhaps, my sweet?'

She'd want to scream,

'*Wake the fuck up, people's homes are being washed away.*'

But he never actually asked about her work. Once, bone weary from the day, she'd tried,

'Don't you ever wonder about what I do?'

Anything to break the impression of living in a Jane Austen novel.

He'd raised one eyebrow in that infuriating manner, his tone one of mild reproach, and said,

'My dear, I'm sure you do it awfully well.'

Then took his pocket watch – a fucking pocket watch! – and uttered,

'Gosh, is that the time? I must retire to my chamber, we're riding with the Athenry Hunt at seven.'

The country was submerged in water but these barbarians insisted on hunting down and allowing a pack of hounds to tear asunder a terrorized fox. She'd jumped up, not quite startling him but definitely getting his attention. His eyes met hers. Usually he'd gaze at a spot just above her right shoulder. She stomped to the drinks cabinet and shouted,

'Jesus Christ, you've every spirit on the planet except Jameson.'

He said,

'There's a rather fine claret I fetched from the cellar.'

She glared at him, wanting to bury him in the fucking cellar. Grabbing a bottle of Glenfiddich, she poured it into a large, beautiful, hand-crafted crystal tumbler. An heirloom from sweet old Mumsie! Turned to him, drained the glass, tried not to shudder when it hit her raw stomach, asked,

'Guess what I got in the post this morning?'

Paused.

'Darling?'

With that tolerant smile as outrider, he answered,

'Not the foggiest, *dear*.'

Her head was awash with

resentment,

rage,

confusion.

She bored into his eyes, said,

'A headstone.'

He was slightly bemused, tried,

'A silly prank, no doubt.'

'*Oh, Christ*,' she thought. She really needed to talk to Jack. Anthony was waiting expectantly, geared for some mildly verbal chess. Her anger drained away. She finished the whiskey, turned on her heel and went to her room. When Anthony's daughter, Jenny, had been around, it had been easier. You could put a Band-Aid on a seeping wound. But the girl was at finishing school in, yeah . . . Switzerland.

Ridge had barely finished any school.

To aid her recovery from the savage beating, to vent her

frustration and to try to restore her shattered confidence, she'd enrolled in a gruelling kick-boxing class. She was next to hopeless for a few weeks and the other students sneered at her. Drove her on. Then one day, it began to click. She took down the best student, and the Master, who claimed to be from Tibet but was actually from Shantalla, actually bowed to her.

Not only did it get her in shape, it emptied the simmering anger. On days when her muscles ached and her spirit cried,

'Stop!'

she'd mutter,

'By all that's holy, no man is ever, ever going to put his fucking hands on me again.'

After the encounter with Anthony, after a fierce day of families in deep distress over the flooding, she was exhausted. Leaving work, her spirits were as low as the final decade of the rosary. She longed for intimacy and her car just took its own self to Devon Park. She thought she'd just sit for an hour, let misery wash over her. Seeing the two regulars walking their dogs began the balm. She thought of Jack. God knows, he was no angel, as maddening as Anthony, but he did listen to her, attentively.

Despite their long decade of bruised, compromising, caring skirmishes, he remained an enigma. As likely to give twenty euros to a homeless person as bring his hurley to a bully. The time a guy had been verbally abusing his young boy in broad daylight, and Jack, oh sweet Jesus, Jack had put the guy through a pane-glass window.

Or those awful days when she'd been terrorized by a stalker, who'd she called?

Jack.

And he . . . took care of business.

Or his stricken face when his surrogate son took the bullets meant for him.

Jesus.

How was he still getting out of bed in the morning?

Or when Serena May went out of the window on Jack's watch. He'd gone to bits, ended up in a mental hospital. And, God knew, he was a hopeless drunk, and, she suspected, addicted to every illegal substance available. But no matter, when your back was to the wall, it was this ageing, hearing-aid-wearing, limping wreck that you called.

And he showed up. Always.

Anthony despised him, not only because of the wrong side of town he'd been reared in, but because of his total lack of respect for his *betters*. Anthony had described him once, in a fit of pique, as an alkie vigilante with notions above his station.

To her eternal shame, she'd said nothing.

Silent affirmation.

In an effort to understand Jack, she'd borrowed some of his mystery novels. Jack was always on about mystery being the literature of the street. No Booker-literature shite for him. Whatever else, Ridge was a cop of the streets. He'd given her James Lee Burke, commenting in that way he had, 'We'll start you at the top, work yer way down.'

Pegasus Descending, a line in that book pierced her soul.

'Marry up, screw down.'

And the titles, like poetry in their own selves:
  In the Electric Mist with Confederate Dead,
  The Tin Roof Blowdown,
and her absolute favourite,
  A Stained White Radiance.

Pushed by an almost irascible need, she got out of the car. So, OK, maybe Jen had a new lover or would simply slam the door in her face. But she had to try. When she reached the path, two guys in hoodies seemed to materialize from the shadows. She saw the glint of a very large knife in the nearest one's hands. She cautioned,

'Whoa lads, back up a bit, I'm a Ban Garda.'

The second hissed,

'You're a fucking dyke is what you are.'

The nearest one lunged, fast. She sidestepped easily, swung around, almost balletic, rammed her right foot in his balls. The second one whined,

'Jesus, no need for that,'

and launched at her.

She did a twirl, enjoying her own self, used a high left kick to smash his nose, followed with a right kick to his gut. Then she was pinned to the ground by the fucking dog walkers! She didn't know whether to laugh or cry. A girl appeared from, like, nowhere, helping the hoodies to their feet, saying to the local heroes, the dog guys,

'She tried to attack those young men, I think she had a knife.'

She could hear a siren in the distance – coming for her?

Ah, for fuck's sake.

10

'A headstone tells you, in truth, nothing of value.'

Stewart

I needed to visit me money. So many banks were going down the toilet and, like the clergy, being exposed to every abuse possible. With Laura arriving soon, I wanted to be able to show her I was – am – viable, at least financially.

I went to my local branch on Eyre Square. I managed to secure a face-to-face with one of the assistant managers. He had a small walled-in space and a very harried look. I put out me hand, said,

'Jack Taylor.'

He was in his mid thirties, with a posture that made him look a hundred. He took my hand, one of those dead-fish shakes. He had his shirt sleeves rolled up – just one of us working stiffs. He said,

'I'm Mr Drennan.'

Mister!

You have to be at least seventy and somewhat affable for me to call you Mister. But I rolled with the play, asked,

'How is my account?'

He had my file before him, peered through it, said,

'You have a very healthy balance, Mr Taylor.'
I said,
'Show me.'
Threw him.
He asked,
'You want to see it?'
'My money, my call.'
He pushed the file over reluctantly.
It was looking good. I was very relieved. He said,
'You are earning very little interest in that savings account. Might I suggest some shares you could buy?'
'No.'
He was confused, asked,
'You don't want to make some money?'
I looked him straight in the eye, said,
'If I wanted to make more money, you think I might have mentioned it? I want to see my money. The newspapers, they seem to think you guys have stolen every euro in the land.'
He looked around, but help was not to hand, tried,
'You'd like a printout of your account?'
Unheard of in banking circles, it seemed. No wonder they were getting away with frigging wholesale larceny.
I sat back, relaxed. You get to fuck with the banks, enjoy.
I said,
'Unless you want to bring me the actual cash – and I have no problem with that, believe me. Put it in a bin liner and I'll stroll out of here as happy as a Galway oyster.'
He rose, said,

'I'll get right on it.'

I don't think he meant the bin liner.

I got the printout and said,

'You need to chill, mate, get out, have a few brews and tell yer own self, 'tis only money.'

He didn't wish me God bless.

No wonder the fucks are in trouble.

It was pissing like a bastard. Rain, that is.

My dad was a lot on my mind those days. Probably the only hero I still had. I'd given up on wanting to be him. But it was a comfort while living in a new land of vultures and predators to think of him. He'd worked on the railways and, to my surprise, taken early retirement. I never asked him about it, but I knew it weighed heavily on his mind.

He'd said to me one time, when as per usual the banks were threatening the wrath of God as our mortgage fell behind,

'Jack, if you owed the bank fifty quid, they'd take the house from under you.'

I never forget that.

I never forget him.

Stewart was sitting in one of the very few authentic vegan cafés in the city. Situated but a lovely grilled T-bone steak from the Augustine church, it was fundamentalist in its strict no-meat policy.

Word was, a guy was turned away for wearing a leather jacket.

Urban myth.

And footwear: canvas was, dare I say, kosher. Stewart was wearing his winter crocs, differed from the summer style in that you wore socks.

A guy telling me about the Irish wardrobe during the summer said,

'Roll up the sleeves on your sweater.'

Stewart was intent on his new venture. Investing in the growing boom of head shops. Legal highs in the high street. He had a wadge of cash invested in one and was fretting about the government threats to close down the loopholes that allowed the shops to sell dope in all varieties. But clouds were gathering. Two students had died as a result of the products and the public were becoming volatile about the epidemic of new outlets.

One had even been burned out in Dublin.

Plus, the dope gangs were mightily pissed off about the loss of revenue this was costing them. He was seriously considering cashing in before the axe fell. That was his main gig, getting out before the shite hit the fan.

A shadow fell across his notes. He looked up. A heavily built man in his fifties was staring at him. He had a face of sheer granite, with old acne scars across his upper jaw. Heavy tissue around his eyes testified to some time as a boxer. The broken nose confirmed it. He was wearing a very smart Crombie coat, collar turned up, with a fedora perched rakishly on his head. He asked,

'Mind if I join you?'

Pause.

'Stewart.'

Stewart nodded and the man sat, his heavy bulk strafing the chair. A waitress appeared, asked,

'May I get you something, sir?'

He gave her a lazy look, full of disinterest, said,

'Yeah, coffee, black.'

He unbuttoned his heavy coat to reveal an ill-fitting brown suit with a puke-green waistcoat.

'I'm Mason. Been looking for your boss, Taylor, but he seems to have disappeared. Probably sleeping off his latest piss-up.'

It took Stewart a moment to grasp the cadence of the accent – British but muted. He answered,

'He's not my boss.'

Mason raised an eyebrow, then said,

'You seriously believe that?'

The coffee arrived. Mason took a sip, spat, asked,

'What the fuck is that swill?'

The waitress beat a fast and faster retreat.

Mason pushed the cup aside, said,

'Trust me, sonny, I've done my research; you're the gopher.'

Stewart applied all his Zen mastery, tried to envisage a sunlit meadow, but the sheer bulk of Mason blotted out the light. He asked,

'Who are you?'

Mason gave a deep smoker's laugh, full of phlegm and venom, reached into his jacket, produced a wallet with a gold badge, said,

'I'm a private investigator. The real deal. Not like your

employer's half-arsed attempt. I used to be with the Met and after retirement took full accreditation as a PI.'

Stewart was tired of the guy, tried,

'And you want to see Jack – why?'

Mason fixed his flat eyes on Stewart, glinting steel, said,

'I've no fucking interest in that has-been. I've been employed by the family of Ronan Wall to look into his disappearance. You're a messenger boy, so deliver this to the alkie. This is my case and he's to keep well clear of it. You got that, son?'

Stewart was still grabbing for some serenity.

Working it wasn't, but he managed,

'Jack has no involvement in that case.'

Mason snapped his wallet shut. You could see the slick movement had been practised before the mirror a lot. He said,

'Good, keep it that way. There's a world of hurt for those who fall foul of me.'

He stood up, buttoned his coat, asked,

'Ex-con, right?'

Stewart didn't feel it warranted a reply and Mason smiled. No warmth had ever touched that smile and it certainly didn't now. He said,

'Good lad. You sniff around my case, I'll have you back behind bars in coke time.'

Stewart had finally found a place, deep within, where he could trust his mouth. He asked,

'Your intimidating manner get you a lot of results?'

Mason had been on the point of leaving but turned back,

leaned right across the table into Stewart's face, his breath an acrid blend of nicotine and belligerence, hissed,

'Dipshit, I eat the likes of you for breakfast. I can stitch you up in ways you'd never imagine.'

Then he patted Stewart on the head, said,

'Now run along, there's a good lad.'

He was done, set to head for the door, when Stewart said,

'I did learn a thing or two in prison. The louder the mouth, the bigger the target.'

Mason laughed, said,

'Next time we chat, I won't be so cordial.'

And was gone.

Stewart tried to imagine such an encounter between Mason and Jack.

Phew-oh.

The Dylan album came to mind, he'd been listening to these old guys at Jack's probing. *Blood on the Tracks.*

11

*'A headstone doesn't end nightmares.
Sometimes it causes them.'*

KB

Ridge was standing before Superintendent Clancy. His main hatchet man, O'Brien, was by his side, smirk in place. Ridge marvelled that once Clancy had been Jack's best friend and was now his sworn enemy. When she'd tried to probe Jack on it, he'd said,

'Shite happens.'

Her alliance with Jack was a continuous black mark in her file.

Clancy kept her waiting, poring over papers, making odd grunts of assent.

Who knew?

He was uttering,

'Hmmph . . . mm.'

By the holy!

Finally, he removed his reading glasses – gold rimmed, of course – sat back, surveyed her. His eyes were pure slabs of slate. He said,

'You were arrested by two citizens.'

She started to say,

'Sir, it was a—'

'Shut the fuck up. Did I ask you to speak?'

O'Brien gave a wide grin. She took some solace in knowing that Jack had once beaten the living daylights out of him.

Clancy continued,

'If the media got hold of this, we'd have a cluster fuck on our hands.'

She longed to say something but bit down,

hard.

Clancy said,

'As a favour to your husband, I'm not going to launch an official investigation.'

He stared at her.

What?

Was she, like, supposed to say, 'Golly gee, thank you so much, yah prick'?

He continued,

'You're confined to desk duty for a month. You can handle a phone, I presume, without aggravation?'

He returned his reading glasses to his vein-burst nose, said,

'Now get the fuck out of my sight.'

As she slunk out, she began to better understand Jack's loathing of the man.

Anthony was waiting outside, dressed like the country squire, all pomp and damn little circumstance. To her horror, she noticed he was wearing his riding breeches as he strode to the BMW, and was that a cravat . . . with the emblem of the Galway Hunt? He barked,

'Get in the car.'

Ridge, never the most tolerant of individuals, already way past her simmer date, asked,

'What?'

He stopped, said,

'We'll discuss this at home. I had to pull a lot of strings to save your pathetic career.'

She ran up to him, got right in his aristocratic face, said,

'Pull this,'

and yanked the cravat from his neck.

Before he could protest she said, 'One fucking word, just one, and I'll make you eat this piece of rubbish,' turned on her heel and walked towards the city centre.

She had to stop at the Wolfe Tone Bridge as she realized her whole world was going down the toilet.

She fumbled for her mobile, her hands shaking, called Stewart. No frills, she begged,

'Can I stay with you for a few days?'

If he was fazed, he didn't sound it. But nothing ever seemed to get to him. He said,

'A Garda in my house? Fantastic.'

One of the reasons she loved him, he never, never asked,

'Why?'

You find a friend like that, they're freaking gold.

That a convicted drug-dealer and a Garda were tight was a conundrum neither of them analysed. Jack had brought them together, but even he never expected they would form a separate peace. They did share one quality, an indefinable regard for the train wreck he was. Each, in their separate ways, felt they might yet save him. When Ridge had begun her martial-arts programme, Stewart had encouraged her, offering Zen wisdom to beat the wall of pain.

Jack, of course, true to form, on hearing of her enterprise, muttered,

'I'll rely on my hurley.'

When Ridge arrived at Stewart's house, he already had a room prepared. His home was on the edge of Cooke's Corner. But only a post-mortem away from the fish shop where a body had been found in the freezer, after it had been there for many years. Of course, the local wits had a field day, the very least of which was,

'Ah, he was always a cold fish.'

Mafia jokes, too, of course, not so much sleeping with the fishes as being on ice with them.

Stewart was dressed in a silk kimono, black with gold dragons. It should have looked ridiculous, like Hefner on ludes. But his smooth, lithe movements and air of total calm carried it off.

He hugged her and she nearly broke down. How long since anyone had done that and truly meant it? She could feel the easy strength of his body. He released her, said,

'Tea's in the pot, toast ready to pop and my special omelette is just the right tone of crisp and delicious.'

He ordered her to sit, served them both breakfast, commanding,

'Eat first, talk after.'

She asked,

'Is that Zen?'

He smiled, said,

'No, that's hunger.'

The omelette was heaven, laced with a hint of spice. She gasped,

'God, this is good.'

He said,

'And not a magic mushroom in the mix.'

Finished, they sat back, sipped the Darjeeling tea, and he told her about the new player, Mason, the official PI. She said she'd run a background check, adding ruefully,

'If I'm still allowed to use the computer at work.'

Stewart wasn't big on self-pity and asked about the attack on her. He considered, moved into a lotus position on the chair, said,

'First Malachy, then a handicapped man murdered, and now you. And one of your attackers referring to your sexual orientation.'

She asked,

'You think they're connected?'

He wasn't sure, said,

'Sometimes you need Jack's crazy view on things. He sees weird patterns that a normal person would miss.'

Ridge nearly smiled. Whatever else, Jack would never be condemned as normal. She asked,

'Where is he? Do you think he's gone on one of those biblical benders?'

Stewart never replied instantly, took all the factors into account.

'A ferocious lash, no. He's drinking, sure, but not in his usual blitzkrieg blaze. Laura, the American woman, is due soon and I sincerely believe he has feelings for her. I'm almost afraid to voice it, but I think he's close to happy.'

Ridge tried to envisage such a concept, said,

'Jack and happy in the same sentence?'

Stewart didn't reply to this, moved like a cat from the chair, offering more tea. Ridge confided,

'One of my greatest fears is going to his apartment and finding he's choked on his own vomit.'

Stewart stopped in mid stride. He'd imagined that very scenario more times than he'd ever admit.

12

'Torture should be inflicted as though completely disinterested. No more than a procedure to be carried through to its brutal conclusion.'

Ex-'freedom fighter'

I cringe when I think how easily they took me. Am I ashamed?

You betcha.

Mortified, in fact. Worse, it made me vulnerable, the worst sensation in the world when all you've got to protect yerself is . . . yerself. Thing is, I'd been busy, oh fuck, like a banshee on a mission. Flush on my result from Loyola's housekeeper, I'd nicked the photo of the cottage and muttered inanities about later visits. She seemed bewildered. Not my problem, least not then. I headed for Monroe's on the end of Dominic Street. Huge place with the great asset of quiet corners. I ordered a Jay, Guinness back. Settled in to savour my triumph. I pulled the photo from the frame and bingo, all me ships coming in, the address was on the back.

Just outside Oughterard. I knew beyond a shadow of a tinker's doubt he'd be there. The loving way the house-keeper had glanced at it, he was there. I drained the Jay in one burst of elation. Told meself,

'*You've still got the moves, son.*'

A hefty draft of the black and I was flying.

. . . In the face of God?

As the old people say.

I was as close to delighted as I'd been since Galway won three All Irelands in a row.

Glory days.

I was having me some now. Muttered,

'I found him, Jesus wept, I did it, cracked the case.' This meant a serious bonus from the lizard Gabriel, and Laura was due real soon. I could afford to have the apartment professionally cleaned.

My mobile shrilled. I signalled to the barman for the same again, answered,

'Yeah?'

'Jack, it's Stewart.'

'How's it going, buddy?'

'You sound very . . . chipper.'

Chipper?

People actually use this outside of British sitcoms?

I said,

'Laura's arriving in jig time . . . and I cracked a major case.'

His voice quickened.

'You found who mugged Malachy?'

Malachy, Christ, I'd forgotten all about him. I said,

'No, but a case with a nice lump of change.'

Silence.

I figured he wasn't counting my blessings. Then he said,

'Malachy too poor to count?'

Sarcasm leaking all over the words.

I was fucked if I'd let him puncture my balloon. Said, with total ice,

'Don't lecture me, pal.'

And God forgive me, added,

'You weren't so damn righteous when you came to me whining about your dead sister.'

I regretted it instantly, knew how horrendous it was. I can't excuse it, it was a low cheap wounding shot. Blame my state of euphoria.

He sounded as maimed as I'd anticipated, said,

'I called to tell you that I'd been checking on Ronan Wall's sister.'

Another case that had dropped way down on my priorities. As I fumbled for a way to erase or stem the pain, he added,

'Ronan Wall is an only child.'

But Bethany, the Goth girl I'd met?

I said,

'What?'

'He doesn't have a sister.'

Clicked off.

I worked on my second pint, considered calling him back and saying . . . what?

Instead, I used my mobile to get Directory Inquiries, got them to connect me to the best pub in Oughterard. It rang a bit, then a gruff voice answered.

'Liam, it's Jack Taylor.'

Another ex-Guard, Liam took early retirement, bought a pub/restaurant. We have some history, most of it fairly good. He needed a moment, then,

'By the Holy, Jack Taylor! I was beginning to think you were a rumour running round as a fact.'

You don't have to be Irish to decipher that, though it helps to remove logic from such conversations. I asked,

'How's biz?'

He sighed, said,

'Sweet Jesus, bollixed. The usual crop of Christmas parties – and they bring in major cash – would usually be booking now, but they're scarcer than a politician with the truth.'

I didn't sympathize. That would be as much help to him as an audit, I said,

'A lady friend and I were hoping to have dinner there this Saturday.'

Jesus, it felt odd to say that, strange and wondrous. To be, in fact, no longer singular.

He laughed, astonished, said,

'There must be a rib broke in the Devil. Jack Taylor finally hooked!'

Now for the lure.

'I was hoping to introduce her to Loyola,' (deliberately omitting the 'Father'; get that hands-on friendship-gig going).

He paused.

Few are as loyal as an ex-Guard, and especially when they are protecting a disgraced priest. Our history was riddled with such precedents. Carefully, he asked,

'You know him?'

Time to kick for the sympathy/guilt trip. I said,

'When my poor mother passed, may she rest in peace, he was a tower of strength, arranged everything. I don't know how I'd have got through without him.'

Dumb fuck bought it.

Nothing like

    priests,

    dead mothers,

    guilt,

to shake the bastards.

He became flustered.

'Jack, I meant to get to the funeral, to send a Mass card, to—'

Enough of this shite. I cut him off at the knees, said, adding a wee sting,

'She always loved you, Liam.'

Then, before he could re-group from that shovelful of polite recrimination, I asked,

'Is he still partial to the old drop of Paddy?'

Anxious to move on, he rushed,

'Oh, Lord, yes. Only yesterday, I made him a hot one.'

Gotcha.

I said,

'Liam, put one of your oldest vintages aside, cost no problem, and don't tell him we're coming. We really want to see the look on his face.'

'Honest to God, Jack, my lips are sealed.'

'See you Saturday, mate.'

Rung off.

Man, I was hitting them out of the freaking ballpark. Sank my second Jay in pure delight. It burned like the Resurrection. I needed nicotine for the best call of all. Settled my tab with the barman and added a twenty for his trouble. He had to know, asked,

'Jack, you're all lit up, you win the Lotto or what?'

I gave him my best smile, said,

'Only the ecclesiastical version.'

More's the Irish curse, I actually believed it. The next day, I'd arranged the cleaning service. They'd be done by evening. I made strong coffee, and it kicked in about the same time as the Xanax. Now for the fun part. I rang Gabriel; he answered on the second ring. I said,

'It's Jack Taylor.'

He replied with a terse,

'Well?'

Boy, I'd be so glad to be free of this shithead. I decided to skip the frills, just lunge in, said,

'I found Loyola.'

He couldn't hide his astonishment, went,

'Already?'

Trying, if not much, to rein in my smugness, I said,

'What you paid for.'

The guy was really up now.

'That is capital. You've done splendidly and more than earned your bonus.'

I gave him the details and location of the cottage. A tiny voice niggled in my head, intoning,

'*Thirty pieces of silver.*'

I put the phone down and the Xanax dissipated my feeling of unease. I focused on Laura; two days and she'd be here. I was excited, as close to happy as it gets. I said aloud,

'Ton of cash imminent, Laura arriving, it's almost too good to be true.'

I should have paid more attention to my own utterance. The cleaning crew arrived, I gave them the spare set of keys and they assured me I'd be able to return by five at the latest. I asked if they preferred cash or cheque and we all smiled at the absurdity of this. Cash it was. To kill the early part of the day, I went to see Kathryn Bigelow's *The Hurt Locker*. Last movie of hers I'd seen had Lance Henriksen in the ultimate vampire/rock 'n' roller.

The cinema was nigh empty: no screaming kids, no groups of eejits with buckets of popcorn. You come out of the cinema alone, there is usually a terrible sense of loss, but hey, I had Laura due, no more ticket for one. I went to Faller's, bought a gold Claddagh pendant for her. Checked my watch. I was doing good, time for a jar or three.

Went to the Róisín Dubh. Had intended to be out of there in time to get back and tip the cleaners. But I got involved in a session, someone started singing 'The Cliffs Of Dooneen' and a guy joined in on the spoons, another with a bodhrán, and we were off and reeling. It was way past six when I staggered out. I decided to take a short cut along the canal. Stopped about a hundred yards up to light a cig, muttering about the amount of litter dumped in the water. Thought I heard footsteps and then received an almighty blow to the base of my skull. Saw the cigarette float down into the water, like a tiny light of hope. Blackness took me as my legs buckled.

I came to with a start and a ferocious fright. I couldn't see. Jesus, was I blind? Took some deep breaths, which worsened an already thundering headache. Then I realized I was blindfolded.

And . . . tied down.

The fuck was this? The DTs in a whole new guise?

My wrists and ankles were manacled and, by moving my body a bit, I knew I was spreadeagled. Not good. A voice, distorted with one of those robot gadgets, said,

'Jack, you're back.'

Behind the metallic sound, you'd have sworn there was concern. He was standing at my head, but once I began to orient myself a bit, I sensed there were others to my sides. He said,

'To satisfy your curiosity, you're laid out on a headstone.'

A pause.

Added,

'Better than under it.'

Laughter from the others. Jesus, a psycho with a sense of humour.

He continued,

'You had a call from an American lady. I hope you don't think we exceeded our brief, but my female colleague answered, said, and I think I quote her correctly,

'*Jack is rather deep in me as we speak, so fuck off home and harass Iraq.*'

Oh, Jesus.

I managed to say nothing, mostly as I had nothing I could possibly think of that didn't involve threats or heavy obscenities and when you're tied down, that's not really the best course of action.

I could distinctly hear him drinking something and I'd have sold a lot for a drop of whatever it was. He said,

'The cunt took the very next flight out. It's none of my business, Jack, but just how devoted to you can she have been when she baulked at the first hurdle?'

I managed to find some semblance of a voice, cracked, hoarse, asked,

'Could I have some water?'

He gave an artificial 'Whoops', said,

'I'm dreadfully sorry, Jack, where are my manners? Of course you can. We're not animals. Sparkling or still?'

Despite the robotic device, something in his terminology triggered a memory. I'd heard this prick before. I'd deal with that later – if there was a later. I said,

'Long as it's wet.'

He laughed, said,

'Ah, that spirit, Jack, is why we love you.'

My mouth was wrenched open, a bottle put to my lips and glorious cold water poured. I coughed, spluttered but got it down. No Jameson tasted as sweet. The voice said,

'Now to business. I think we share a dislike of chit-chat.'

A hectoring tone now behind the device said,

'As a lover of America, I think you'll appreciate our somewhat altered version of the following.'

He took my silence as assent. Intoned,

'Give us your wretched,

'your poor,

'your infirm,

'your dregs,

'your outcasts.'

Stopped, said,

'You get my drift?'

I managed,

'How fucking complicated is it?'

He gave a bitter laugh, said,

'That's my boy, bitter and vicious. We've added our own little kicker. Would you like to hear it?'

I croaked,

'I have a choice?'

Received a sharp vicious jab to my kidneys, with a bat . . . a baseball bat? It hurt like be-jaysus. Heard, soon as I got my wind back,

'We're being nice here, Jack, but we can do hardball too. Are we clear?'

I managed,

'Crystal.'

'So, would you like to hear our addendum?'

'Yes, I would.'

'Okey dokey, after the rigmarole of "Give us your scum" and such, we've added,

'And we'll annihilate them.'

Sweat coursed down my body.

He continued,

  'Misfits,

  'retards,

  'gays,

  'the parasites.

'Oh, yes, I nearly forgot, especially for you, Jack,

  'alkies.

'We shall cleanse the planet of them. Recognize anyone familiar in there, Jacky boy?'

Total silence reigned for a few blessed minutes, then in an almost jolly tone he said,

'But Jack, *hermano*, buddy, you're sweating like a bloody pig.'

Maybe the worst thing of all, in this horror show, he touched my cheek with two fingers almost caressingly, said,

'Chill, big guy, we're not ready to take you off the board . . .'

A single beat, then,

'Yet.'

Chills and sweats were running down my back, my hair was literally saturated from panic. It was about to get worse, a whole lot.

He said,

'We have a rather fascinating dilemma for you. You get a choice, not unlike *The Dice Man* or *Sophie's Choice*. I mention books to help you de-stress.'

Guess what? It wasn't helping.

He said,

'I need to know first, though, which hand do you drink with?'

Without thinking, I said,

'The one that shakes the least.'

Received a second stunning blow to my gut that was so fierce I threw up – threw up the water and some other stuff I don't think I want to know. I stuttered,

'My . . . right . . . right hand.'

'Just one more question, buddy, and we're nearly done. Would you prefer to read or drink?'

Where the fuck was this lunatic going? I said,

'To read.'

I think that's true.

He said,

'Good choice. Blinding you would be a trifle messy, so just bear with us a minute.'

My right hand, manacled, was gripped, pinned down, my fingers forcibly spread. I heard,

'Stanley knife, please.'

13

'Applause is finite.'

KB

I came to in a hospital bed. For some bizarre reason, with an old proverb in my befuddled mind.

Only dead fish swim with the stream.

Shaking this off, I tried to get a handle on where I was. Then the previous events came slithering back and my whole body went into a spasm. I tried to sit up.

Stewart, perched in an armchair, moved fast, said,

'Best to lie still, buddy.'

Buddy?

He ever call me that before?

Fuck, meant I was in serious bad shape. I took some deep breaths, trying to fend off the tidal wave of panic about to engulf me. I asked,

'Could I have some water?'

He gently put some ice cubes in my mouth and nirvana, they tasted so fine. I lay back, refusing to look at my right hand. Between the glorious coldness of the ice, I asked,

'How'd I get here?'

He moved back to his chair, never taking his eyes off me, said,

'They had your mobile phone, found my number, said—'

He hesitated.

I pushed,

'Spit it out, Stewart.'

He swallowed.

Maybe he could use an ice cube?

Said,

'They said, "We've left the garbage outside your door."'

I suppose they could have recycled me.

He continued,

'Ridge has been staying with me. You've been missing for nearly a week.'

I asked,

'How are Chelsea doing?'

He looked so ill at ease, no Zen gig helping, it seemed, so I cut to the chase, asked,

'How bad?'

I didn't mean my football team.

He inhaled deeply.

'They took two fingers from your right hand. They'd, ah, cauterized the . . . remains, otherwise you'd have bled to death.'

A chill ran down my spine, but I had to know.

'Did they leave the digits – the severed ones?'

Oh, Christ, the freaking desperate hope that they did and that the surgeons had done their magic and re-attached them. Stewart looked stricken. I said,

'I guess that's a no.'

It was.

He said,

'Ridge is working round the clock, trying to find a lead.'

My mind, maybe in an effort to save whatever tattered remnants remained, muttered,

'*The moving finger writes; and, having writ, moves on.*'

I nearly laughed.

Hysteria?

You bet your arse.

I asked,

'How is Malachy?'

He shook his head, said,

'No change.'

Then he did a thing that broke every rule Stewart held close. He moved over, lit a cigarette and said,

'You'll be wanting some of this, I'm thinking.'

I've always had some incomprehensible bond with him, but I swear by all that's holy, I fucking loved the guy right then. He said,

'The nurses will massacre me.'

I nearly smiled, said,

'Jesus, they'd need to be quick.'

The cigarette done, he took the stub, extinguished it, put it in his jacket. Opened a window to let the smoke disperse. Either that or he was going to jump. He waved his arms futilely, said,

'You caused quite a stir, Jack. The Guards were here. Even Clancy showed up.'

Venom washed over me. I said,
'No doubt he wept.'
Then I zoned out – it was to be like that, in and out of
consciousness, lucid one moment, stark raving mad the
next. I heard, as if from a great distance, a poem by Marin
de Brun, based on Dalton Trumbo's book *Johnny Got His
Gun*. The lines uncoiling in my head like a soured mantra:

> Sightless, soundless
> Your day's begun
> Tearless, wordless, no songs be sung
> Your hand in ruins
> your head in hell.

Snapped back to hear Stewart say,
'Clancy said it was self-mutilation, that your self-loathing
had reached boiling point.'
I said,
'It's a theory.'
Maybe it was the nicotine, maybe Clancy, but I finally
looked at my heavily bandaged hand, asked,
'How long before I get out of here?'
'Few days, but, Jack, get some rest, OK?'
I thought,
'*Rest in peace.*'
Before he started on the bullshit of:
> they can do great things these days,
> lots of artificial appendages,
> etc.

I told him,

'They had me spreadeagled on a slab of granite, said it was a headstone.'

I could see the dots connecting in his head. I said,

'Stewart, be real careful, you hear me?'

Rarely to rarest did Stewart allow his real feelings to surface. Zen kept the six years of prison under wraps and the death of his beloved sister, too He utilized that deathly calm to block out the torrents of lethal rage simmering. Wore a mask of amused detachment to keep the world behind metaphorical glass.

Not now.

Fury wrapped his face. His eyes were slits of sheer menace. He said,

'I hope to fuck they have a run at me.'

The nurse came, did that plumping of pillows they do, then gave me a shot. Hurt like a bastard.

Stewart said,

'I'll be back later, Jack. Here's your mobile, it was in your jacket.'

I was slipping back into sleep, said to Stewart,

'They answered the phone to Laura, said enough to send her fleeing back to London.'

He looked truly sorry, said,

'Ah, no, that's just the bloody pits.'

Which is one way of seeing it, I suppose.

I might have phrased it a little more heatedly.

I kept hoping, praying, that somehow, in some wild flight of a miracle, Laura would write to me, and I could then try, try to explain to her what happened.

After he was gone, as my eyes closed, the nurse asked,
    'Is he your son?'
Ah, for fuck's sake.
Before I could rise to indignation, she said,
    'Good-looking lad.'
Then in that blunt way that Irish women have, she asked,
    'Is he married?'
I was messed up enough to lie that he was gay, or say he was married, but I went with,
    'I'll put in the word for you.'
She beamed, said,
    'And I'll get you a sleeping pill this evening.'
Trade off?

14

'I'm not afraid of dying, but I'm absolutely terrified of dying with a pink teddy bear.'

Barbara Ehrenreich, *Smile or Die*

Ridge was sick to her soul at what had happened to Jack. Stewart had told her as gently as he could, but there isn't really a way to soft-soap the severance of fingers. He told her, too, about Laura, and Ridge wept. She had thought that, just maybe, Jack might be happy. Recently, she'd had a check-up to see how she was doing after the radical mastectomy. She loved the book by Barbara Ehrenreich on positive thinking and the so-called PC brigade who waxed fucking lyrical about the positive aspects of cancer. The do-gooders who saw cancer as a makeover opportunity. Barbara was her new hero. All the pink ribbons, pink freaking badges made her so furious. Now, at last, here was a writer saying that those who preached that cancer sufferers could be cured by developing the right attitude, as they peddled shitloads of pink garbage, books, DVDs, T-shirts, added insult to life-threatening injury.

She fingered her gold miraculous medal round her neck, given to her by her late mother. God, she had adored her mother. A strong woman who, as she lay dying, said,

'Alanna, don't put me in a hospice.'

She didn't.

Allowed her the dignity of dying at home. Her mother had fought alcoholism and every other battle in a poor family's life. She'd had, as they say,

'A hard death.'

Near the end, she had gripped Ridge's hand, whispered,

'Be beholden to no man.'

In light of Ridge's sexual orientation, this seemed unlikely, but, working as a Ban Garda, she had to take shit from men every day. Despite Jack's numerous flaws and faults, Ridge felt her mother would have liked him, said perhaps,

'He has a good heart.'

As for Ridge's marriage, she didn't want to think what her mother would have made of that.

Not much.

Ridge knew for certain she would have described Anthony as

'A poor excuse of a man.'

She read on. Stewart was upstairs, doing Zen exercises, no doubt.

He was just finishing his regime, as it happened. Took a moment to dwell on Ridge. He was quite stunned at how well they lived together. He'd been so long on his own, he was, as the old people say, set in his ways.

But she blended right in. Was fine company, knew when to talk and when silence was the best communication. He finally had an eager student of Zen and, in return, she was demonstrating her kick-boxing routines to him. He admired her litheness and her ferocious passion to heal her body and make it strong again. He didn't ask how long she intended to stay as he really didn't care. He'd miss her if she suddenly left, that he knew.

He'd met her husband a few times and found him to be *an empty vessel*. Stewart, like Jack, didn't really do friends, but he would put his life on the line for either Jack or Ridge – and had.

He was selecting some casual gear. His casual gear was all top of the range. He opted for Japanese jeans – read, small fortune – his Ked trainers and a silk T-shirt.

He heard the post come through the letter box. Ridge shouted,

'I got it.'

He was dressed, ready to move, when he heard her scream. He rushed down the stairs. Ridge, sitting on the couch, was ashen, the remnants of an open parcel before her. A small wooden box in the centre of the package. He picked it up and recoiled.

Two severed fingers.

Ridge stared at him, her eyes wide with shock. Then she indicated a pristine white card. He picked it up, read,

Garda Ni Iomaire, A touch of Taylor for you so you can, dare we say, finger yourself. Nice display of the martial arts the other evening. Perhaps we can sever your legs when we take you next time. Send a leg to your husband, let him have a piece of meat, too.

Oh, what a gay delight
xxxxxxxxxxx
Headstone.

Ridge buried her head in her hands.

Stewart, for the first time since the awful day he'd been sent to prison, wanted to bury his head in the sand.

He'd been about as ill prepared for jail as possible. Who is? But some adapt fast and learn the basic rule of survival.

Eat or be eaten.

That day in the prison van – the Paddy wagon they called it – manacled to some thug who'd raped a young girl, the judge's sentence ringing in his ears:

'*Six years, with no possibility of parole.*'

Stewart had been a designer dope-dealer, believing – well, kind of believing – that he was a different sort of entrepreneur.

Yeah.

Had bought his own scummy act, just supplying what the people wanted, and had his own rules.

Jesus.

Like that made it different.

He didn't deal in heroin. As if all the other shite he peddled wasn't lethal. That was how he met Jack Taylor – one of his regulars. He knew he was in deepest shit when, during process, the guard said,

'Pretty boy, I give you a week before you top yourself.'

And the thug he'd been manacled to had giggled,

'They'll run the train on you, nancy boy.'

He learned fast that the train was serial rape and the train ran all the long day. He took some severe beatings, which in a bizarre way stopped him from suicide.

Who had the time?

When they're kicking the living hell out of you at every moment, who had the energy to kill themselves? He'd have gone under, no doubt, just wrapped his neck in those wet sheets and let it swing. Then his sister was murdered.

And everything changed.

Stewart didn't know about love then, but he did know he adored his sister. It was like a click in his head, the warden telling him,

'Your sister killed herself. Probably so ashamed of you.'

He didn't go after the warden. He went to the yard, walked up to the train head honcho, said,

'Any last words?'

The guy and his crew laughed, laughed a lot. Here was this yuppie, a wannabe player, giving them cheek. The guy spat on Stewart's prison-issue sneakers, said,

'You going to off me, that it, yah little queer?'

Stewart wondered why they not only aped American gangsters but spoke like them, too. Stewart glanced around at this guy's crew, said in a calm, level voice,

'I'm going to kill him now, then, day by day, I'm going to kill each and every one of you.'

The laughter had eased a bit. This wasn't your everyday occurrence, a nerd calling out not only the most dangerous guy on the yard but threatening his whole team.

The guy, his smirk less smirksome, asked,

'What you got, homie, beside your head up your arse?'

Stewart used the palm of his right hand to slam the guy's nose all the way to his brain. Killed him stone dead, turned, said,

'One down.'

No recriminations, no payback. The warden figured if the worst guy in the prison got taken care of,

good.

Then he waited in his cell for hell or Armageddon. He was the most lethal kind of man now. He just didn't care, and that vibe leaked its way to the crew who were clamouring for his head.

Day One . . . threats.

Day Two . . . silence.

The third day, a guy appeared in his cell, said,

'Enough.'

Stewart, working on marine exercises he'd found on the internet, paused, asked,

'Is it?'

The guy was nervous, they'd never come across such a case. How do you deal with a man who truly doesn't care? He tried,

'We want to call a truce. Nobody will bother you and, if you like, we'd be glad to have your back.'

Stewart wanted to shout,

'Stop with the pseudo-American bullshit. You fucks tried to have my back all right.'

He said,

'I'll give it some thought.'

And so began his Zen education.

He devoured everything he could on the subject and then got in touch with Jack Taylor. The broken-down PI solved his sister's murder. For that, Stewart would always be in his debt. In a hugely over-populated prison system, Stewart remained solo. No one, not one con, would cell with him. He got a makeshift desk, hung above it the following:

> In the hour of adversity
> be not afraid
> for
> Crystal Rain falls
> from
> Black Clouds.

He worked out every day.

Hard.

Till his body screamed,

'Enough.'

Then he worked it some more.

Devouring Zen like a famished peasant, he no longer thought in terms of the six years he'd serve. He thought only of discipline.

The day finally came when he was due to be released and he had to face the warden for the obligatory pep talk.

He had his bag of meagre possessions, the grand sum of twenty euro from his brief stint working in the mail room.

The warden, sitting behind a massive pine desk, said,

'So, you're to be a free man.'

Stewart toyed with the Zen idea of saying,

'*No man is free who thinks thus.*'

But thought,

'*Fuck it.*'

Said,

'Yes, I am.'

He knew he was supposed to add, 'sir,' but he'd served every day of his time so he didn't have to do shit. The warden didn't like it, said,

'You passed up every chance of a parole hearing, time off for good behaviour. You want to share with me why that was?'

Stewart said,

'No, not really.'

The warden was close to apoplexy, said,

'I could have you here for some more time if I wished. You are aware of that?'

Stewart said,

'Of course, and if you do, I'll be obliged to divulge the young kids you personally entertain.'

The warden was on his feet, his face red and bulging from temper. He shouted,

'You'll be back and, trust me, I'll see to it that you have my personal attention next time.'

Stewart gave what was to become his personal trademark, a languid smile, and said,

'I very much doubt that. I'd like to give you something to remember me by.'

The warden, perplexed, said,

'I think I'll remember you.'

Stewart turned to leave. He was now free. Threw a tiny package on the pine desk, said,

'Relish.'

It was much later in the evening, a few Jamesons to the wind, when the warden finally opened the package, his hands trembling slightly, and out tumbled a scrap of toilet paper, with these words:

'What you don't see with your eyes, don't witness with your mouth.'

Ridge was sobbing. Stewart moved to her, put his arm round her, said,

'I know some people, I'll have them keep watch on Anthony.'

Stewart wasn't much of a drinker but he kept booze in the house. Never knew, Jack might arrive. He went to the kitchen, poured a large glass of Jameson and added sugar, for the shock, brought it back to her, and held it to her lips till a sizeable dent had been put in it.

Waited.

He had, of course, every drug known to man, but she needed to have the trauma eased and fast.

Finally, she composed herself, said,

'I'm not as tough as I thought.'

He smiled, said,

'None of us are.'

Then added,

'It's not about toughness, it's about strength.'
She asked,
'Zen?'
'No, just the truth.'
She averted her eyes from the carnage on the table, said,
'They're like ghosts in the wind. We'll never find them.'
Stewart, fighting like a dervish not to let his simmering anger show, said,
'They've made two major mistakes. The first was setting a pattern that we can trace.'
She waited, then asked,
'The second?'
'Not killing Jack when they had the chance.'

15

'Vulnerability is akin to victim theory.'

Graffiti

I had the usual professionals come and, as the Americans say, visit. They had the obligatory psychologist who, I shit thee not, said,

'This will require a period of readjustment.'

I was like a bastard. They'd cut back on my painkillers. I asked,

'For us both?'

He'd obviously been clued in as to what I was like and gave that tolerant smile, said,

'Anger is part of the process.'

So I said,

'Then you won't be surprised at my next line.'

He continued with that emphatic smile, asked,

'Yes?'

'Fuck off.'

Was he delighted?

Yeah, I think so.

He continued in that soothing tone they use for muzak interludes,

'You've been through a traumatic experience and time is needed—'

I cut him off, asked,

'How would you know?'

He had doe eyes, and a mop of hair that he continually flicked back, annoying the hell out of me. He said,

'Believe me, Mr Taylor, I've worked in this field for many years.'

I asked,

'They've a field for Stanley knives?'

Lost him for a sec but he rallied.

'We have many modules for coming to terms with such events.'

I said,

'Cutting your balls off – which module would that come under?'

He stared at me. I continued,

'That's what I thought they were going to do.'

He stood up, said,

'Perhaps another day when you're less . . .'

He reached for the euphemistic adjective, settled for '. . . stressed'.

I sat up in the bed, asked,

'What's your name again?'

Like I could give a flying fuck.

He said,

'Dr Ryan.'

I held up my bandaged right hand, said,

'See this? They sliced off my fingers. How many days

you figure for me to de-stress every time I look at it?'

He fucked off.

Next up was the woman who spoke about the wonderful strides in artificial aids. I let her yammer on and she took my silence for interest, finally wound down, asked,

'Which appendage do you think you might be most interested in?'

I said,

'The one that allows me to swing a hurley.'

Threw her. She said,

'I don't follow.'

But I felt she was truly trying to help, so I went easy. Well, easier. Said,

'I'll get back to you.'

The nurses liked me.

Actually that's a lie.

One did.

She enjoyed the run-around I gave the high-falutin' consultants, said,

'You're a terrible man.'

I agreed.

She had some edge so I liked her. Anything to get away from the freaking platitudes I'd been listening to. She said,

'You're fierce cranky.'

I said,

'Give me a few shots of Jameson, I'm a teddy bear.'

She had a great laugh. I love women who laugh with their whole body, not worried if their mascara will run. She said,

'From the look of you, I'd say you've had your fair share of that devil.'

Any mention of the Devil tended to quiet me: too many bad memories of an individual who might/might not have been the Anti-Christ in person.

Any further discussion was deferred when she said,

'You have a visitor.'

Caz, a Romanian who managed to avoid the periodic round-up of non-nationals for deportation. Ten years he'd been in Galway and had learned, as Louis MacNeice wrote, 'all the sly cunning of our race'.

And I figure he was no slouch to begin with. He'd even acquired a passable Galway accent and was more native than a Claddagh ring. I never knew if we were friends. He was too elusive, but we'd known each other a long time and had an arrangement:

I'd give,

he'd take.

But he was one of the most reliable sources of gossip in a city that thrived on stories. Add to that, he worked with the Garda as an interpreter for the Romanian community, so he had the ear of the powers that be, sort of. True, he was as trustworthy as the eels that swam in the canal, but I liked him.

Mostly.

He was dressed in a Boss leather jacket. I recognized it as my surrogate son had once given me one. Both were gone.

And a white sweatshirt with the logo 'Don't Sweat It'.

He said,

'I'm sorry about what happened to you, Jack.'

'Thanks.'

He reached in the fine jacket, said,

'I brought you something.'

Now I sat up, this was a first, said,

'If it's fucking grapes, I'll strangle you with the fingers I've left.'

He produced a half-bottle of Jay, checked the door, handed it to me and my left hand. I said,

'Take the seal off.'

He did.

I drank deep and gratefully, handed the bottle to him. He still had the moves, didn't wipe the neck – that's class. He took a fairly decent wallop himself, grimaced, said,

'*Sláinte.*'

We waited a few minutes to let the Jay do its biz, warm the stomach, promise false hope, and then he asked,

'How bad is it?'

'Two fingers.'

He nodded. He'd literally escaped from a country that was awash with every atrocity known, so two fingers weren't as stunning to him as to your average citizen. We had another drink, the bottle going back and forth like we were two settled friends. I gave him a brief outline of the Headstone outfit and he pledged to ask around. The Jay and an earlier shot of morphine were taking their toll and he stood, said,

'It pains me to see you hurt, my friend.'

I think he actually meant it.

I hope I said thanks.

I do remember he squeezed my shoulder and said,

'For now, rest. Later, we'll extract the vengeance of the Romanian.'

And I did – rest, that is.

Till I came to, a single night-light burning near my bed. I'd dreamed of my dad and Laura.

One of those awful dreams that's so real you can taste it. Everything is OK till you wake and . . . it ain't.

My dad was holding my hand, looking at my fingers, soothing, saying,

'They'll heal, son, don't worry.'

And Laura, she was in the distance, her hand held out, saying softly,

'But Jack, you have no fingers I can hold.'

Yeah, like that.

Jesus wept and then some. I think there were tears on my face, but I don't know. Loss is sometimes so palpable you can almost touch it.

Almost.

The night-light threw an eerie glow across the room. I struggled to sit up, still half caught in the desire of the dream, phantom pain in my destroyed hand, and my heart did a jig as I saw a dark figure rise from the chair in the corner. Maybe the light-bringer was back to claim his own. He stood, moved into the dim radiance, and I thought,

'*Yeah, the Devil, all right.*'

16

'Being afraid is natural.
Being afraid to do something about it
is an insult to life.'

KB

Father Gabriel.

Looking immaculate as usual. If the Pope can wear Gucci slippers, then no reason why Gabe shouldn't have his clerical suit made by Armani; it had that cut. His white collar seemed to gleam in the half-light, matching his perfect teeth and discreet tan. He moved like an athlete. He leaned over me, asked,

'How are you, Jack?'

Like he gave a good fuck.

I said,

'Been better.'

He made the sign of the cross over me. I wish I could say it was a comfort but, from him, it was more like a curse. He smelled of some great aftershave. Man, this guy was a player.

But at what?

He said,

'The Brethren have been praying for you.'

What? That I'd croak?

I nodded, trying to appear appreciative. He reached in his elegant jacket, produced a fat envelope, left it on the bed, said,

'Your bonus. I think you'll find it more than generous.'

I asked,

'You found Loyola then?'

He gave a radiant smile, providing more illumination than the measly night-light, said,

'Your information was spot on. A job well done. Your Church will remember the great service you performed on its behalf.'

I pushed,

'So, what happens to Loyola now?'

The smile was still in place but it had eased. He said,

'Back in the flock. All is well in God's world.'

Fucking guy didn't get out much, it seemed.

He added,

'Now, Jack, don't concern yourself any more with that. You must focus on recovery and bask in the task you did so admirably for Mother Church.'

He was so slick, so polished, you could almost believe him. I kept at it, though.

'The money that Loyola nicked – got it back, I guess?'

He touched my shoulder, said,

'Jack, you fret too much. Be assured, all is restored.'

His touch was like the grip of a cobra, the venom just waiting to be spat, and his eyes had hardened. I asked,

'You ever read Tim McLaurin?'

The tolerant smile. He said,

'Oh, Jack, if only we all had the time to read as much as you, but no, I haven't.'

I figured accounts sheets were more his forte. I said,

'*Esse quam videm.*'

He finally released the grip on my shoulder, leaned back, said,

'Latin? I should really know the meaning, but one's memory is not what it was.'

This fuck remembered how much he got on his First Holy Communion and who gave what. I smiled, said,

'Don't fret! It means "to be, rather than to be seen".'

He considered that.

'Meaning?'

'My doctor, Dr Boxer, told me that and my meaning is, do I get to see Loyola? Let's call it a vested interest.'

I nodded at the fat envelope, continued,

'Be nice to actually meet the dude who got me such a fine payday.'

He looked at his watch. Yeah – you guessed it – not a freaking Timex, a fine slim gold job, said,

'I must run, Jack. I'll try and visit soon.'

And he was gone.

He made no sound as he slipped from the room. A clerical stealth bomber, and no doubt, this guy was incendiary. I glanced uneasily at the envelope. I should be delighted. Few things give me the blast like counting money, especially if it belongs to me. But the term 'tainted' rooted in my head. Something was off centre and I knew in my heart, that, whatever else I'd done, I hadn't, as he'd said, performed a

great service for Mother Church. Betrayal touched my
tongue like blood in my mouth.

My favourite nurse came in to settle me, said,

'Isn't that a lovely aftershave? What is it?'

'Treachery.'

She looked at me, said,

'The names they give new fragrances these days. Men are
getting better aromas than women.'

Like I'd know.

She had gotten me a sleeper and I said,

'You're an angel.'

'Ah, go away with that. You wouldn't know an angel if it
flapped its wings in your face.'

But I did know their opposite number – and all too
fucking well.

She plumped my pillows, saw the envelope, said,

'You got a card?'

I didn't answer and she asked,

'Are you all right, Jack? You seem down in yourself.'

'I'm good, honest, just a bit weary.'

And wary.

After she'd gone, I did count the money. It was a lot; an
awful lot.

I was due to be discharged in a few days but I caught an
infection which developed into a fever and I was semi-
comatose for another two weeks. I dreamed a lot of Laura
and my surrogate son, and would come to, bathed in sweat,
my heart hopping in my bedraggled chest. Sorrow was like

a constant cloud over me and lashed me in every way it could. Times, too, I woke to an irritating itch in my hand and no fingers to do the necessary, and despair loomed larger than at almost any time in my banjaxed existence.

I do remember a patient strolling into my room a few times. I think his name was Anthony but I wouldn't swear to it. He liked to sit and read the papers aloud, saying,

'Keep you up to date with what you're missing.'

What, like my fingers, my fucking life, Laura?

I'd drift in and out of fever as he read on.

One particular morning, as the fever was finally abating, was reading as usual. I'd missed the first few lines but caught:

'. . . *medals to the families of Captain Dave O'Flaherty, Sergeant Paddy Mooney and Corporal Niall Byrne. The Minister said, despite adverse conditions, the crew had responded with the Air Corps search and service motto . . . GO MAIRIDIS BEO (that others may live). The Minister deeply regretted the shameful length of time it had taken to acknowledge their sacrifice. The Bakers said, "We don't wish for a medal for our son. It won't compensate for the cover-up and the mishandling of the affair."'*

I really believe that piece moved my recovery onwards; the cover-up lingered in my mind. If heroes – as those amazing men were – could be doubted, it was time for me to get my act together and get out of there.

17

The Brothers Grimm

Jimmy and Sean Bennet, the worker bees of the Headstone crew, were born to wealth – not quite in the same league as Bine, but definitely in the neighbourhood. They'd gone to the same flash boarding school as he did, but he was a few years ahead and he shone in sports, grades, popularity. The golden boy. The brothers, alas, didn't shine in one single area, save surliness. To their amazement, the senior boy, the wunderkind, took an interest in them.

He approached them one day as yet again they sat miserably on the football field, unchosen. He said,

'Guys, you wanna go smoke some weed?'

His accent was quasi-American and as likely to change as his mood. They didn't know that then. He led them behind the locker rooms, produced some serious spliffs, offered them over, said,

'Fire 'em up; let's get wasted.'

They did.

He spouted a lot of shite about superior races, Darwin, and making your mark. They agreed with everything. He told them he had a nice supply of dope available and needed people he could trust.

Sean, stoned but still aware, thought,

'*Runners.*'

But, what the hell, they'd do anything he asked; he was the guy.

Time came, they got busted – rather, Bine did and laid it off on them. They took the rap and he promised one day in history he'd repay.

History they were.

Expelled.

Bine went on to college and some dark sun continued to light his way.

The brothers, failures at just about everything, were given a trust fund and basically told to 'Fend for your miserable selves.'

They had the money so they got an apartment and spent their time eating junk food, doing dope, watching slash movies. They'd almost forgotten Bine when he called round to their apartment one day. Ignoring the squalor of the place – empty takeaway cartons, sink afloat in unwashed dishes – he said,

'See, I told you guys I'd be back and your day would come.'

He was dressed in black: combats, sweatshirt, Doc Martens. Embraced them both. It was a long time since any person had touched them in any way. He said,

'The day has come, my crew.'

If he noticed the shithole they were living in, he didn't

comment. No one else did either as no one else ever came. He produced a bottle of Wild Turkey and a nice bundle of nose candy. Said,

'*Mis amigos*, get wasted and then we'll talk.'

They did some serious lines, washed down with the bourbon in heavy dollops. They were sitting at the battered remains of what had once been a valuable antique table; not any more. The brothers had seen to that. Bine sat back, said,

''Kay, here's the gig. Firstly, I want to ask you guys a question. Your miserable lives going anywhere?'

Jimmy took the insult easily, he was used to it, but Sean didn't much care for it. He said,

'We have some plans.'

Bine threw back his head, laughed loudly, scoffed,

'Right, like watching Tarantino, Rodriguez movies, eating fast food and doing weed.'

All true.

Bine added,

'Like to be in your own real-life movie, make a real name for yerselves, get splashed on the front pages of every paper in the country?'

Sure. Who wouldn't?

He said,

'But the thing is, it takes *cojones* to make that kind of impact and I wonder if you guys have what it takes.'

Sean said,

'Bring it on.'

Bine gave a glorious smile, said,

'Simple test.'

Jimmy, wanting to keep current, said,

'Yeah, what you got?'

Bine reached into a battered holdall, pulled out a gun, said,

'See this? It's your real Colt .45. My old man paid a fortune for it. Take a look.'

It was black, shiny and for all the world like the one Clint used in his Westerns.

Jimmy said,

'Fucking beauty.'

Bine produced one single bullet, inserted it and spun the barrel, said,

'Here's where we see what you got.'

He put the gun to his head, pulled the trigger.

Click . . . *nada*.

He inverted the gun, handed it to Sean, barrel first, asked,

'Wanna play?'

Sean didn't even think, analyse or swirl the barrel, put it to his head, pulled the trigger.

Click . . . *nada*.

Then grabbed the Turkey, drank straight from the bottle.

Bine said,

'My kind of guy, like Clooney said in *Dusk till Dawn*. You are in my cool book.'

They turned to Jimmy, whose whole life was a movie; he just wished he had a bandana so he could be Chris Walken in *The Deer Hunter*. He took the Colt, made a dramatic show of spinning the chamber and then put it to his head.

For one lucid moment, Sean nearly cried,

'Fuck's sake, STOP!'

He didn't rate much in the world of bile and hatred he inhabited. But Jimmy, Jesus, Jimmy was all he had, and . . . without him?

The gun cocked and, almost in slow motion, the hammer came down.

Click . . . not this day.

Sean realized he was sweating and Jimmy whooped,

'Fucking A, way cool, dude!'

Bine smiled. He had the two stupid bollixes in the palm of his brilliant hand.

He said,

'Group hug, guys, you passed.'

Sean wasn't wild about this shite but went with it. Bine laid out some celebratory lines, said,

'The family that cokes together, croaks together.'

Jimmy thought that was hilarious.

Bine straightened up, the coke hitting him fast, said,

'Here's the plan.'

Laid it out.

Jimmy would have agreed to anything, but Sean thought it was way out there. Bine said,

'Now we begin. Jimmy, your first job is to go to a grave-yard and get us a headstone.'

Sean was beginning to think he was in a movie by Sam Raimi. He asked,

'A headstone?'

Bine moved to his feet in an easy, almost elegant way, said,

'From now on, we have to have certain rules. One, you don't question my orders. Two, I say jump, you ask, how high?'

Sean was thinking,

'*Like fuck.*'

Bine tossed the Colt to Sean, said,

'My gift to you and Headstone. It's our name and it's where we are going . . . to lay every fuckhead this side of the Shannon.'

He then went off on a rant about the losers, the scum, the parasites, and how they personally would make a statement to rid the country of all the flotsam.

What snared Sean was when Bine asked,

'You had some dealings with a so-called PI named Taylor?'

Jesus, Sean was shocked. How could he know that?

The fire of rage that burned in Sean for that man. A few years back, Sean was, he thought, doing good with a babe in a nightclub. Sean ever doing anything with a girl was a non-starter and so, OK, she was protesting, but Sean was flying on dust when this bouncer, an ex-cop, filling in for that one night, grabbed him and said,

'You wanna be a rapist?'

Him? Sean . . . Rape?

And in the middle of the club, he had beaten Sean mercilessly, to the jeers and delight of the clubbers. And then had dragged Sean literally by his hair – very long then – to the door, put his shoe in his arse, said,

'I see you again, I won't go so easy.'

Before Sean could ask anything, Bine said,

'He's on the list.'

Sean was sold.

Later, Sean would realize that Bine knew exactly what buttons to press for whoever he needed. It was like a black gift.

Bine ranted on again about Darwin and superior races and a lot of stuff that Sean tuned out of, till Bine said,

'There's another member of our crew.'

The brothers waited for the revelation.

But Bine was thinking how much these two eejits reminded him of the Mendoza brothers. Not that it mattered.

Much.

He never intended them to survive C-Day anyway, and if by any chance they did, he'd off the stupid fucks himself. Jimmy he regarded simply as fodder, but he didn't much care for the looks Sean gave him. Time to sweeten the pie. He said,

'There's a girl – sweet, sweet wee fang.'

Sean nearly groaned. The rants were easier to listen to than the awful American twang.

He let that sink in.

Jimmy simply drooled. Sean waited, so Bine continued,

'Name of Bethany, but don't let her gorgeous body fool you. This is a lethal fox. You diss her, she'll have your balls for a bracelet.'

He reached in his jacket and Sean thought,

'*What, he's got, like, a photo?*'

It was a list.

He said,

'I want that last taken care of asap.'

Then threw a shitload of euros on the table.

Jimmy was thinking, *'Takeaway pizza,'* Sean was thinking, *'Phew-oh, large-denomination notes.'* Bine said,

'Where was I? Oh, right, Beth. She's my fuck buddy, but you guys do right by me, I'll give you some of that sweet meat.'

Finally, he put a Stanley knife on the battered table, said,

'Use this as much as possible. Call it a sentimental quirk.'

He made to leave, paused, said,

'Keep this in mind.'

He paused again for effect, then said,

'More rage, more rage. Remember what our guys said: it's humans I hate.'

He looked at Sean.

'Look it up, you're a bright kid.'

As he got to the door, he added,

'Here's a hint. *We're going to kick-start a revolution, I've declared war on the human race and war is what it is.'*

He withheld the other part of that rant:

'You guys will all die and it will be fucking soon.'

18

'Revenge Tango.'

Jerry A. Rodriguez

It's quite difficult to get beaten up in hospital. I mean, apart from the Saturday-night war zone of the A & E. That's open season, as the skels, the drunks, the dopers, the crazies show up. Not to mention the arrogance of the consultants who verbally cut you to shreds at every opportunity. Despite the array of marauding infections, if you actually have a bed, you are reasonably safe.

You'd think.

Right?

I was almost fully recovered from the virus I'd picked up and was feeling, if not exactly healthy, at least less battered. Lord in heaven, I'd even managed some nights' sleep without aids. Day before my discharge, I woke, or rather was dragged from my sleep. A burly man had a ferocious grip on my pyjama top and was hauling me upright. It took me a few moments to grasp this was real, not part of the recent fever. I tried to focus and then recognized Liam, the ex-guard who owned the pub in Oughterard. I'd phoned him about Loyola under the pretext of booking a table at his restaurant and quizzed him as to the fugitive priest's location. Reluctantly, he'd confirmed that the cottage was indeed Loyola's and that he was in residence.

Liam was one of those old-style cops you rarely see any more. Big, built like a shithouse and rough as be-jaysus. He'd been a fierce hurler, one of the best, and we'd played together a few times. He took no prisoners, ever. Regular methods of policing held no interest for him; his fists were his investigative technique.

His face was testament to his career: bruised, nose broken many times, a face mottled by rosacea and a riot of broken veins. He drank like he played hurling. Like a lunatic. Spittle leaked from his lips as he shouted,

'You lying piece of shite, Taylor!'

As a wake-up call, it sure beats tea and toast. It gets you wide awake. Fast.

Before I could speak, he drew back his mighty fist and smashed it to the right side of my face. It bounced me off the bed frame. He was about to follow through when he noticed my emaciated chest through my torn top. He pulled the punch. When my head cleared a bit, I gasped,

'What the hell did I do?'

He considered that second punch, said,

'You phoned me, you treacherous bollix, got me to confirm Loyola's home.'

I tried to pull together the tattered top, grab if not dignity at least a wee modicum of decency, asked,

'So, what's the big deal?'

Bad, bad mistake.

He punched me in the kidneys and I'd have thrown up my breakfast if I'd had any. He spat,

'You told somebody and guess what? Guess fucking what, Mr Private Eye? Three days after I talk to you, that lovely man is found floating in the river outside his cottage.'

I muttered,

'Sweet Jesus.'

He moved back from the bed, having caught sight of my mutilated hand, said,

'They say your fingers were sliced off.'

Delicately put.

He was spent. I guess kicking the living shit out of a half-dead guy in a hospital bed has its drawbacks. He said,

'You know, Jack, I used to like you. You were always as odd as two left feet, but I thought you had some principles.'

I tried,

'What a terrible accident for that poor man.'

Jesus, he nearly blew again, roared,

'Accident! Accident, my arse.'

I didn't know what to say. My right cheek was already swelling and I knew from past experience I'd have one beauty of a black eye. I mumbled,

'I'm sorry.'

He was at the door, said,

'I'm sorry, too. Sorry they didn't cut your balls off.'

Two days later, finally, I was released. Ireland was coming to the end of a freakish three-week period of freezing ice and snow. People had broken hips, fractures, from slipping on footpaths deadly with black ice. The government had imported salt from Spain.

Fuck, I knew we were short of most everything, especially irony, but *salt*?

Come on.

The salt was to cover the roads.

Schools were closed, water rationed, pipes burst or frozen. We'd already entered the Apocalypse.

You don't get to leave hospital without stern diatribes from a doctor. Mine warned me about the phantom feelings I'd have in my lost fingers. I nearly said,

'*Rubbing salt in the wounds?*'

Went with,

'All my feelings are ghosts anyway.'

He stared at my now impressive black eye. I said,

'I fell out of bed and, no, I won't sue.'

He, God bless him, prescribed some heavy painkillers, cautioned,

'Avoid alcohol while taking them.'

I'd have winked but my eye still hurt.

They insist on wheeling you to the door in a wheelchair to see you safely off the premises. Break your arse on the ice outside, they couldn't give a fuck. Stewart was waiting outside, dressed in a fetching Gore-Tex coat with a Trinity scarf wrapped round his neck. He didn't go there, but then, who did? I was so glad to see him, but did I show it? Did I fuck.

He said,

'I asked the hospital to notify me on your release.'

My legs were unsteady from disuse and my limp had

roared back with a vengeance. First thing, I lit a cig. Stewart frowned and I snapped,

'Don't fucking start.'

He sighed, said,

'The car is over here, I'll swing it round.'

I began to walk, slowly, badly, but doing it. Dizziness from nicotine, the cold, freedom, jostled to land me on my arse, but I stayed, if not steady, at least moving. I said,

'I'll be in the River Inn, and who knows, I might even buy you lunch.'

The ice was even worse than I expected and it took me twenty minutes to manoeuvre the short distance. Getting in there – ah, bliss. The waitress who'd served Gabriel and me what seemed a lifetime ago – certainly Loyola's lifetime – exclaimed,

'By all that's holy, Jack, what on earth happened to you?'

I said,

'I got religion.'

She was well used to not understanding a word I said, but she liked me anyway. Led me to a corner table and I ordered a large toddy. She said,

'And why wouldn't you? And this is on me.'

Such people kill me. Give me the arseholes, the head-fucking-bangers, the predators, and I can function, but a truly nice person . . . it makes me want to weep.

I was settled in a comfortable chair, watching the wind rage outside, the hot Jay before me, trying to prise the top off the painkiller tube, when Stewart arrived. He took it all in but said nothing. On the good side of the hot spirit, the pills doing their alchemy, I let out my breath. Stewart, watching me like a dejected Siamese cat, asked,

'How'd you get the black eye?'

'The nurses didn't like me.'

He nearly smiled, then told me about the continued apparently random attacks on the frail and vulnerable. I said,

'Let me guess, the victims are all different from so-called *ordinary* citizens?'

Those Zen eyes allowed a small surprise. He said,

'Go on.'

I told him of the speech the bastard had given me before he used the knife. He stared at me, said,

'Close your eyes for a second, visualize the scene.'

I finished my drink, my stomach already warm and fuzzy, asked,

'Are you out of your fucking mind? I'm trying like a banker to blank out the whole thing.'

He persisted.

'Do you trust me, Jack?'

Jesus, what a question.

I didn't trust me own self, never mind anybody else.

Fuck.

Before I could utter some lame shite like 'Sure . . . but—' he held up his index finger, said,

'This will be brief, I promise. Focus on my finger and then hear me count from ten.'

I thought,

'*Bollocks.*'

And then – whiteout.

Literally.

Where did I go?

What happened?

To this bloody day, I've no idea. One of those terrible ironies of alcoholism, striving for numbness and terrified of losing control.

What the Brits call a *conundrum*.

Great word. I might actually understand what it means someday.

Stewart was tapping my shoulder, saying,

'You did great; it's done.'

Took me a moment to re-focus. I wasn't in hospital, unless they'd installed a bar on the wards, and I didn't rule out the possibility. I wasn't being tortured, and felt pretty OK. I asked,

'What did you do?'

He shrugged, no biggie, said,

'Just a mild hypnosis.'

I asked,

'Did I give up my ATM number?'

He nearly smiled, said,

'You remembered a name, the name of the guy who gave the ethnic-cleansing speech.'

I was impressed, asked,

'Who is he?'

'Bine.'

I nearly choked, spluttered,

'Bine, that's it? The fuck kind of name is that?'

He was deep in thought, held up a hand, the equivalent of *Sssh*.

Which I love.

He said,

'It triggers something. I'm not quite there yet but I'm so close.'

My waitress brought us over two toasted sandwiches, said,

'You're skin and bone, Jack.'

Looked at Stewart with a blend of interest and amusement, said,

'Don't worry – yours is vegan.'

He gave her his rare smile. When he did – smile, that is – he looked like a kid, a nice one, and it lit her up. He said,

'Thank you so very much.'

I swear to God, I'd known her a long time and now she . . . blushed.

She said,

'Ah, 'tis nothing.'

The winning smile again from my Zen maestro.

'Generosity without expectation of recompense is true spirit.'

I could tell, like meself, she wasn't entirely sure what the hell he meant, but she loved it; me, not so much. Seeing him revealed, at least a bit, prompted me to tell him about Laura, or maybe I was simply maudlin. He seemed truly sorry, said,

'Isn't there any way you can fix it? I'll go to bat for you, tell her what happened.'

I shook my head. Some things you can't fix. I switched channels, asked about Malachy, he said,

'Still comatose.'

For all his Zen masks, I knew him – knew there was something. I pushed.

'What else, Stewart?'

He tried a bite of the sandwich, liked it, wiped his mouth then took a deep breath, told me about Ridge receiving the fingers. I had no answer. None that didn't involve deep obscenities, profound insanity. I desperately wanted another drink, but in deference to him, I didn't. He described the attack on Ridge, too, then he suddenly sat bolt upright, said,

'The girl. The girl who asked you to find her brother . . . what's his name?

'Ronan Wall.'

He was cruising into it, asked,

'Describe her.'

I did.

He digested that and whatever wheels were turning in that eerie head of his were at full speed. He said, almost to himself, the sandwich forgotten,

'Bine . . . abbreviation for?'

I took a bite of mine; it was good, hint of garlic on the meat and my favourite, mayo. I told myself, soaks up the booze, so got to be good.

He said,

'When they made the attempt on Ridge, there was a girl,

A Goth type, and she sounds a whole lot like the girl you just described under hypnosis.'

Time for me to add something. I said,

'This group, I figure, four core members. Worse, these attacks, I think they are only a foretaste of the main event.'

'Like what?'

'I don't know. They could easily have killed me when they had the chance. But, let me think, OK? It's like they're holding me for the main event. That make any sense to you?'

It didn't.

So I blundered on,

'The girl, always the girl. I have a gut feeling, we find her, we bust this maelstrom wide open.'

The pills, the booze, the food, being out of hospital, suddenly ganged up on me. I gasped,

'Jaysus, enough.'

And I couldn't stifle a huge yawn.

Stewart stood, said,

'C'mon Jack, let's get you home, back to your apartment.'

We left a large tip for our waitress, and I could be wrong, but did she slip Stewart her phone number? And fuck, God forgive me, worse, was I jealous?

19

'Headstones signify a lot of profound thoughts but a drunk on Quay Street said they meant, you're beyond fucked.'

KB

At Nun's Island, as we got out of the car, Stewart said,

'Just a second.'

Opened the trunk and took out three large grocery bags. I asked,

'You're moving in with me?'

He sighed, said,

'Felt you might need some provisions.'

It was such a decent thing to do; you'd be delighted at someone's care.

Right?

I was wondering if there was booze in there. Fuck the other crap. He carried them up the three flights of stairs, too. Opening the door took a time, as we had to literally push it due to the stack-up of mail. The usual free offers, pizza vouchers, notification of winning millions of euros – and a letter from Laura; I could recognize her handwriting.

There are lines from the insane prose poem 'Literary Heroine' that go

I swear I'd have read your letter dying,
But alas, it was lost, among the debris of the slow and lying.
It's the reason why your letter and my life, so softly
Slip away
Un-noticed least by me.

I stared at the letter for a few minutes until Stewart asked,
'You going to open it?'
I told the truth, said,
'Maybe later.'
I turned the heat on full and Stewart marvelled,
'The place is spotless. I'd have thought – sorry, Jack, but it would be like a . . . you know, a bachelor pad.'
Translate . . . filthy.
I didn't tell him about the professional cleaners. I reached in my jacket, got the envelope Gabriel had given me and let the contents spill on to the coffee table. A turmoil of large-denomination notes littered the surface, swirled to the carpet, a whirlwind of blood cash. A treasure trove of treachery.
Stewart gasped, muttered,
'They paid you for being in hospital?'
I could have laughed. He asked,
'How much is it?'
'A lot.'
Stewart began unpacking the goods, asking if there was a special place for things.
I gave him the look, he figured, *no*. I went to the overhead cupboard, pulled down the Jameson and said,

'I'm fresh out of herbal tea, unless you bought some.'

Fuck, he had.

And brewed it up. It smelt like vinegar gone south. He'd bought cookies, the healthy ones, the ones they manage to remove everything from, especially the taste. We imbibed our separate feasts and Stewart asked if I'd like him to cook up something.

I said I was good, the sandwich had been plenty. The latent control freak that he was, he began to pick up the money and I near shouted,

'Don't.'

He stopped, a hundred note resting in his hand, and asked,

'You like to see it spread out, yeah?'

'No, I like to see it on the floor, where it belongs.'

Finally, he said he'd better make a move and asked,

'You going to be OK, Jack?'

I said sure and thanked him again for the hypnosis feat, reiterated it was very impressive.

He stopped, said,

'Jack, there's all sorts of things I could help you with.'

He had an eagerness I was loath to puncture, but that never stopped me. I said,

'Yeah, you mean that?'

His face lit up. He said,

'Just name it, Jack.'

'Restore my fingers.'

I saw the pain in his eyes as I shut the door.

I went to the fridge, pulled out an ice-cold bottle of

Hoegaarden, that fine blond imported beer that we can never pronounce, and got the top off with my left hand. Figured I might as well get familiar with that hand, it was in for a lot of use. I drank some of the beer chased with the Jay and felt, if not better, at least energized.

Time to get ready for action. Some years ago, I'd run into a serious hard case named Kosta. His nationality was never established. I'd done him a major service. He was the real deal, never needed to shout the odds about his nature – his complete ease with violence showed in his eyes. We shared the same ideas about justice and had become almost close. He was a good guy to have in your debt. I was about to call it in. Rang him. He'd told me on our last outing, a messy affair that I'd blundered our way out of, that his gratitude was infinite, saying,

'Jack, anything you ever need, you got it, my pledge to you.'

Right. Let's see how much smoke he was blowing.

If I was American, I'd have him on speed dial. I laboriously tapped his number from my land line, using, yeah, my left hand. I kept telling myself, Kosta dealt in everything on one condition: it was under the radar, i.e.:

Illegal,

Discreet.

He answered on the third ring with '*Kalimera*.'

Greek today, then.

I said,

'Kosta, it's Jack . . . Jack Taylor.'

'*Madonna mia.*'

That's what I heard, or something like it, but it had warmth. I can recognize that in any tongue. I remembered then, he was one of those rarities I'd helped who actually liked me. He said,

'My friend, I am so happy to hear you. They tell me bad things have been done to you.'

I said,

'Why I'm calling you, buddy.'

I remember introducing him to the collected works of Tarantino and he was fond of quoting from the movies. Worked for me and, I guess, Tarantino. Never missing a beat, he said,

'Give me their names Jack, I'll go biblical on their ass.'

I said,

'Thank you, I need a Mossberg pump.'

Not exactly something you can ring up Tesco and order, least not yet.

No hesitation, he said,

'Give me your address, I'll swing by round seven.'

My kind of guy.

And seven, on the dot, my bell rang. I'd managed to grab close to five hours' sleep, popped some Xanax, and was, if not aware, at least alert. I opened the door. He was a small man with a heavily weathered face. Now my own face, I've lines you could plant spuds in, but Kosta made me look young.

Kind of.

His head was shaven, he had an aquiline nose, or so he

said, and large brown eyes that went to black in a nano-second. He was in his perennial black-leather coat and a bespoke suit, like an out-of-work KGB agent. That was not an impression he discouraged. As I knew from our previous form, he spoke Russian fluently.

He grabbed me in a bear hug and was one of the few who I could not only tolerate it from, but feel he meant it. A large sports bag swung loosely in his left hand, with the logo *Ti Krema*.

I'd asked before.

It was Greek for 'What a pity.'

I hadn't asked further. Who in his right frigging mind would?

I welcomed him to my home, and before I could offer hospitality, he unzipped the bag, produced a bottle of Grey Goose. Handed it to me and said,

'Nice place, Jack.'

I asked,

'On the rocks or neat?'

Silly question.

I poured two large, no ice, and said,

'Sit and let's catch up.'

We clinked glasses and I got there first, toasted,

'*Sláinte mhaith*.'

He loved that. Responded with,

'To better days, my dear friend.'

Glanced at my mutilated hand, commanded,

'Drink.'

I did, we did. Ferociously.

He sat back on my freshly cleaned sofa, looked round, said,

'Very clean, very neat; this I like.'

A few moments later, the Goose bit and that warm glow lined my stomach. He stood, glass in hand and began to move around, paid full attention to the bookcases, selected the poems of Hemingway, said,

'I did not know he wrote poetry.'

I said,

'Take it, then you decide if he did.'

He smiled; that's the kind of answer he liked. He pointed his glass towards the sports bag, said,

'Your merchandise is in there.'

Paused, a vague smile hovering, added,

'With ammunition, of course.'

I took out the Mossberg and for a moment I was amazed at how light it felt. He said,

'The barrel, the grip have been sawn off, so it fits almost like a handgun.'

He chuckled, quipped,

'Taylor made.'

Delighted at his own pun, he freshened our drinks. He said,

'Give me the shells.'

I placed half a dozen on the table. They were heavier than I'd imagined. He indicated the gun and I tossed it to him; he caught it effortlessly in one hand. Looked impressive and showed a deep familiarity with the weapon. He muttered,

'*Efharisto poli.*'

'Thank you,' in Greek.

I think.

It didn't mean he was Greek – he liked to use a smattering of several languages – simply that he knew how to say thanks in that one. He flipped the gun to his left hand, grabbed two of the cartridges and inserted them, pumped the barrel once, said,

'Rock 'n' roll.'

Handed it back to me, a man who treated a loaded weapon carefully, a man who knew his trade, said,

'Practise with your left, over and over again, using your right hand to prop the barrel.'

I tried, fumbled, and he moved his finger, i.e., *again*.

I did.

Knowing there were shells in it kept me focused. We stayed at it for a time, his eyes never leaving the weapon. Finally, as sweat began to roll down my face, he signalled: enough. I went to put the gun aside and he said,

'No, make it part of your hand. Until it is, you are an amateur.'

Lesson over, the steel left his voice. He asked,

'Need back-up?'

I thought about it, said,

'Maybe.'

Then I reached for a thick envelope I'd readied and moved to put it in his hand. He shook his head, said,

'No, but perhaps, a little further along, I might call on your assistance.'

I assured him with

'Ask and 'tis done.'

Words that will haunt me to my grave.

We sat, sipped our drinks in more relaxed fashion. Laura's letter was unopened on the table. He asked,

'A woman?'

'Yes.'

'Do you love her?'

With Kosta, everything was direct to the point of bluntness. I said,

'I had hoped I might.'

He pondered that, staring at the remains of the vodka in his glass, said,

'*Quel dommage.*'

That I knew. French for 'what a pity'.

I asked,

'Like a brew to go with the Goose?'

He nodded. Still cradling the Mossberg, I grabbed two ice-cold Buds from the fridge. Screw-off tops, which is, in my view, damn smart. Handed one to him and said,

'To all the girls we loved before.'

He was a major Willy Nelson fan and the duct with Julio Iglesias was a staple on his soundtrack, inner and outer.

He smiled, said,

'And to those who might yet find us old guys ... colourful.'

Unless beige came back into vogue, I was shit out of luck.

He took a large gulp of the brew, waited, then,

'Jack, you were a policeman but you didn't carry a gun.

Now you are not a policeman, you do. Is that how you define irony?'

I said,

'More like insurance.'

His mobile shrilled. He took it from his coat, answered, said,

'*Habla.*'

Listened, his face expressing nothing until he spat out a staccato of some East European language. Then he snapped his phone shut, said,

'A rumour, without a leg to stand on, will find another way to move around.'

I left it, cryptic as it was.

He stood, took me in a bear hug again, said,

'We have much in common, *hermano.*'

Thanked me for the book, the hospitality, and was gone. I drank the Bud slowly, took one of the painkillers the doctor had provided. I wasn't hurting but felt it coming on. Then I lifted Laura's letter, moved over to the sink and, using my Zippo, set it alight. If I opened it, her words would be branded for ever on a soul already too heavy. It burned quickly, like my aspirations, as I held it over the sink. The slightly smouldering remains floated towards the drain like the dying dance of a disintegrating dream. Turned the tap on full, the jet of water sucking the embers of what might have been. I'd laid the gun on the counter top and avoided looking at it lest I put the barrel in my mouth.

I thought of *A Moveable Feast*, of all the wood that had surrounded us then and how I never touched one single piece of it for luck. Blinded by love and joy, I'd believed I'd little need of luck and that Paris would simply continue in Galway and that Laura would hold my hand for ever. One glorious moment, as we were standing by the Eiffel Tower, I'd been looking up at the steel girders when Laura kissed the nape of my neck; a fleeting kiss, almost imperceptible, and my whole body was alight with awe that such a single gesture could have me believe I was bulletproof and that the future would be writ as it was then. A light rain had begun to fall and Laura turned her face up to it, said,

'Thank you, Lord.'

I said,

'Wait till you see the rain in Galway. It's incessant but soft, like your eyes.'

She'd never feel the Galway rain and I'd never feel her gentle eyes light on my face.

Och Ochón . . . Oh misery is me.

I moved back to the sofa, the gun resting in my arm again, turned on Marc Roberts' new album, the track 'Dust In The Storm' killing me slowly. My mobile rang, thank Christ.

20

'A Dhia, tá brón orm.'
('God, I am so sad.')

Old Irish prayer

Stewart.

He launched,

'Father Malachy has regained consciousness.'

Father!

I never . . . never heard Stewart call him thus.

I said,

'Good, how is he?'

Stewart seemed momentarily lost for words; Malachy had that effect. Then,

'I think the nurses might be about to blacken his eyes, too.'

I might actually help them. I asked,

'When can I go see the oul' bastard?'

'Ridge has the day off on Thursday and asks if she can pick you up then, go with you?'

I laughed, not out of humour, but Ridge? Said,

'Safety in numbers. You think we need that for him?'

Without hesitation, he said,

'Actually we were both thinking of protecting him from you.'

Nice.

I needled,

'You think I'd assault a priest?'

'Why not? You've assaulted everyone else.'

The sanctimonious little prick. I hissed,

'Thanks, Stewart, your Zen spirit has made a contented man very old.'

Silence, then,

'Jack, you OK? You sound a little . . . off.'

I thought of Kosta, said,

'I'm all right; as right as a rumour.'

Clicked off.

I crashed early, meaning I managed to get to my bed, took the Mossberg with me – long as I didn't shoot meself during the night, I was doing OK.

Next morning, thank Christ, I couldn't remember my dreams but they'd been rough. When you wake, your hair drenched in sweat and panic riding roughshod all over your torso, you haven't been dreaming you won the freaking Lotto.

Got a scalding shower done, a lethal strong coffee in me and the Xanax. Spent an hour practising the moves with the gun. I was clumsy, couldn't get into a rhythm but stayed with it; it would come. By fuck, I'd make it. Got my all-weather coat. The right inside pocket was a shoplifter's dream, large and unobtrusive. The Mossberg slid in like sin.

I got a yellow pad, wrote down all I knew about Headstone. Took me a time; writing with your left hand for the first time is a bitch.

Done, I sat back, drained the coffee and stared at the pad, willing it to speak to me. There was a pattern, a design; I just hadn't got it yet.

I brushed my teeth, the smell of burnt paper still lingering in the air, hovering above the sink like some spectre of paradise lost, a lost plea of transcendence.

Shrugged on my coat, the gun in place, and headed out to face the day. Whatever it brought, I was at least locked and loaded. As I opened the door, I glanced one last time at the sink and my dead dream, muttered,

'Smoke, that's all.'

I came out of my apartment building, made a sign of the cross at the cathedral, moved across the Salmon Weir Bridge, and didn't look to see if the salmon were jumping. The water had been poisoned two years now and the only things jumping were me nerves.

Of course, I ran into a wise guy, some fuck I vaguely knew, who immediately stared at my fingers, said,

'Not paying your debts, eh?'

It did flit across my mind to have him jump where the salmon didn't. I said,

'Yeah, how'd you know?'

Smirk in place, he said,

'Common as muck these days, everybody's in debt and having to give up parts of their life they never expected.'

I said,

'I gave them your name, said you'd cover my tab.'

Whatever he shouted after me, it contained not only invective but a sense of alarm.

Good.

Books.

I needed to ground myself and nothing, not even the Jay, does it quite like books. I don't always have the focus to read them but I sure do need them around. Especially as a woman was not on the cards, not any more. I headed for my second home.

Charlie Byrne's bookshop has grown and become almost on a par with the swans of Galway as an essential ingredient of the very pulse of the city. I hadn't been since my most recent *accident* and felt almost content to be heading there. I passed the newest head shop, doing, it seemed, a brisk trade. Not a high away was the Oxfam shop, emanating a mellow vibe. And then Charlie's. Sylvia Beach would have been proud of those guys.

Vinny was behind the counter, chatting animatedly to a customer. He had that Clinton touch of making each person feel they were the most important one. His trademark long black hair was trimmed. He no longer resembled John Travolta in *Pulp Fiction*, whose character was named . . . Vincent.

Go figure.

He handed a stack of books to the customer, said,

'Sure, pay the rest when you can.'

Why the town loves the shop.

He saw me, asked,

'Jack, it's my smoke break, time to join me?'

Oh, yeah.

He has the laid-back gig down to a fine art without working it, and yet, if the situation requires it, he can focus like a hunting Galway heron. He lit up his Marlboro Light, offered the pack, and I said,

'Thanks.'

Forgetting, I tried to use my right hand with the Zippo and, without a word, Vinny leaned over, fired me up. I folded my right hand in a feeble fist and asked,

'Want to know?'

He reflected, then,

'On reflection, no.'

Not that he didn't care. It was the very caring that doused his curiosity. He said,

'A friend of yours was in the other day, the Ban Garda?'

I was stunned, asked,

'In an official capacity?'

He laughed, said,

'Jack, we're a bookshop, not a speakeasy.'

Added,

'Least not yet.'

He finished his cig, extinguished it carefully in the bins provided, said,

'She bought a stretch of James Lee Burke.'

Wonders never cease. I muttered,

'Ridge buying books.'

He corrected, gently,

'Bean Ní Iomaire, Jack.'

One of the girls stuck her head out the door, shouted,

'Vin . . . phone!'

I smiled, said,

'Bet you have them primed to do that after five minutes.'

He laughed fully and he has one of those great ones, makes you feel good simply to hear it. He asked,

'How'd you know?'

I said,

'It's what I'd do.'

Now he did glance at his watch, left to him by his late beloved dad. He asked,

'You living in Nun's Island?'

Surprised me and I said in a tone heavier than I meant,

'Keeping track of the customers, that it?'

It was unwarranted and I instantly regretted it. His eyes changed, the usual merriment faded, he said,

'No, it's called keeping track of friends.'

In a piss-poor attempt at reconciliation, I handed over a list, said,

'Any chance you got any of these?'

Ten authors on there:

   Jim Nisbet

   Tom Piccirilli

   Craig McDonald

   Megan Abbott

   Adrian McKinty

And

   Others.

You want to truly offend an author, list them under 'Others'.

He scanned it, said,

'*Fifty Grand* was terrific, the others, apart from *Print the Legend*, I'll need some time on.'

I took out my wallet. Vinny gave me the look, said,

'I didn't get them yet.'

Money just doesn't buy you out of a cluster fuck; ask Tiger Woods.

One last lame salvo. I said,

'We'll have that pint soon.'

He nodded, went back into the shop.

I stood there, mortified. Maybe Vinny's watch, my stupid mishandling of one of my oldest and closest friends, resurrected a painful memory.

My father, Lord rest him, had all his life, over his bed, a portrait of Our Lady of Perpetual Help. After he died, I'd been spending some time with a guy I regarded as a friend. By some odd serendipity, his father was terminally ill. In what I believed to be one of the few decent acts of my befuddled life, I gave the picture to my friend. Not easily, as anything to do with my dad was beyond sacred to me.

The man lingered on for two more years, painful ones, and during that time my erstwhile friend, like so many others, had become, if not my enemy, certainly somebody who avoided me. No surprise there; business as usual, really. My life of alienation even then was in full flow.

Few weeks after the man's funeral, I received a parcel. It contained the portrait and a terse note:

> Jack
> I'm returning this as my father has no further use of it. Not that it did him a whole load of good. We are never going to be friends, Jack, and you know, I doubt we ever were.

There was more; it didn't get better.

But that's what I recall and I remember being gutted by the gesture. To return a holy picture seemed to be an act of desecration. I gave the thing to charity. What had been holy above my father's bed had mutated to utter malice.

I didn't understand the act then, I don't understand it now. For a man like me, always rapid to anger, to flare-ups, I don't think for one single moment I felt even a twinge of anger, only sadness.

Outside Charlie's now, I stubbed my cigarette under my boot, fuck the bin, turned up the collar of my Garda coat, and, as the very last line of Padraig Pearse's poem goes, went my way,

sorrowfully.

21

*'An easier exercise is to look for evidence
rather than jump to conclusions.'*

Detective's handbook

I managed a day without much booze, cut way back on the pills, and so when the morning of Ridge's arrival came, I was, if not clear-eyed, at least mobile. You take what you get. As I waited and sipped at a strong coffee, I practised over and over with the Mossberg. I was getting there. It began to feel like an extension of my arm. That I thought this was some sort of achievement is a fucking sad depiction of how narrow my world had become. I blamed it on the loss of a love almost reached.

Guy like me, who the hell is going to give the dancer's choice?

I felt Laura's loss like the departure of an aspiration you'd yearned for but never seriously considered.

To try and exorcise this demon of woe, I kept glancing at the notes I'd made on Headstone.

Something.

Just nagging at the edge of my mind.

Nope, couldn't get it.

Yet.

Ridge arrived promptly as said. She was dressed in a navy tracksuit with white stripes and looked good, very. She handed over a package, said,

'This was at your door.'

No fucking around. I opened it fast, I was sick to death of bad mail. It contained a glove; flesh-coloured material, and a soft gel-like substance filling two fingers. I tried it on and the gel seemed to almost solidify, yet was flexible. I held up my hand to Ridge, said,

'See, good as new.'

Trying not to let the sheer bitterness leak through the tone.

There was a brief note:

Concealment comes in many guises.

Kosta.

Stewart would have loved the Zen echo.

Ridge, awkwardly, asked,

'Is it comfortable?'

Nothing wrong with a pun, especially when you live in a country that is being rapidly flushed down the toilet.

I punned,

'If the glove fits.'

Ridge took a rapid look at the Mossberg and, before she could start her Guard tirade, I lied,

'It's a replica.'

Did this fly?

Did it fuck.

Her face turned melancholic then and she said,

'Stewart told me about your lady friend. I'm truly sorry, Jack.'

Jack!

Shite, how sorry was she?

I went the full Irish, said,

'God knows, you've had your own troubles.'

She simply nodded, didn't volunteer more, so I let it slide, asked,

'You want some coffee, tea?'

'No, thank you, let's get moving.'

Her car was new, a powerful Audi. She said,

'It's Anthony's.'

Then added in that tone that only a woman can,

'For now.'

I kind of liked that,

I certainly never liked the Anglo-Irish prick anyway.

She was a fine driver, careful, confident and with a force that hinted, 'Do not fuck with me.'

She asked, switching gear, literally,

'How do you think Malachy will be?'

That was a given. I said,

'Like a bad bastard.'

She nearly smiled.

I added,

'He'll also still be scared, so expect him to be even more feisty than usual.'

She risked a look at me, asked,

231

'Is that how you handle . . . fear?'

I shook my head, said,

'The reason God gave us hurleys.'

She pushed,

'Are you talking from personal experience? I mean, about the fear and bad temper?'

Too easy.

I told her the truth, see how that would go.

'I'm bad-tempered naturally – my mother's legacy. Fear makes me dangerous.'

But play the game. You ask questions like that, deep stuff, the least you can do is expect a lobby back and I did, asked,

'What about you, you ever afraid?'

We were nearing the hospital and she swerved neatly to avoid a taxi, said,

'Sometimes I think I was born terrified.'

Deep.

I waited and, sure enough, she added,

'Women have one trait in common with horses.'

Now there were so many easy awful bad responses to that, I just shut the fuck up, waited. She said,

'We both know early on, we are . . . prey.'

Maybe I was deflecting my own answer, so I asked,

'And how do you deal with the fear? I mean, you personally. Horses at least can run.'

She was sliding the powerful car smoothly into a space just vacated, seemed as if she didn't hear me, then as she cut the engine, she turned to me, gave me the full blast of her wide blue eyes, said,

'Not with replicas.'

Of course, I hadn't brought the Mossberg to the hospital. I wasn't intending to shoot the grouchy priest, but maybe . . .

We got out of the car. It was so reassuring to see my right hand appear whole. Total illusion, but isn't damn near everything? What can bear deep scrutiny? As we walked towards the main entrance, I veered to the right, saying,

'Hold it a moment.'

I moved towards a shed. The smokers' latest quarantine. Ridge scoffed,

'You can't be bloody serious. Malachy just came out of a coma, you can't possibly believe?'

I gave her my best smile, part humour, mostly malicious. Dared,

'Want to bet?'

We entered the shed. The thick density of the smoke made it nigh impossible to distinguish anyone. It was like seeing wisps of spirits trailing IVs, shrouded bodies on the precipice of a low-key volcano, I said to Ridge, she of the newly acquired James Lee Burke addiction,

'Ghosts of the nicotine mist.'

Then added,

'There's our boy.'

Sitting on a rusty bench was a caricature of the man we'd both known. He'd aged ten years and lost a shitload of weight. He'd never been a poster boy for any health board, but now he looked like he was waiting his turn to be put in a wooden box. I hailed,

'Malachy.'

He looked up, his eyes so far back in his skull they could only be seeing inwards. He said,

'Taylor, the Devil in person.'

He was obviously intact, so far as his bitterness went. He bellowed,

'What do you want?'

Apart from hitting him on his stubborn head? Then he saw Ridge, changed his tack completely, tried to stand, said,

'*Conas atá tú?*' 'How are you?'

I wondered if he'd be so fucking cordial if he knew she married a Prod. I tried to help him to his feet but he shrugged me off, took Ridge's arm.

How lucky I'm not sensitive. We got him back inside, smoke trailing behind him like the worst of the tabloids. He had his own room on the third floor. In a hospital where people lingered on trolleys for days, it showed the Church might be under attack but it had lost precious little of its clout. It's not so much the Church minding their own as keeping them out of sight.

Ridge helped him into bed. A massive crucifix hung over his bed, and, with any luck, would come crashing down – God coming to him, so to speak. Ridge did the nurse gig of plumping his pillows, setting them so he could be upright. The top of his pyjamas was open, exposing a thin chest, bones jutting and covered with sparse grey hair. A very old battered scapular was intertwined among the hair.

That got to me. Moved me in ways I would never analyse, at least not this side of a bottle of the Jay. I reached in my

Garda coat, handed over a 7Up bottle. He regarded it with withering disdain, said,

'A mineral, that's what you brought? I hate fizzy drinks.'

I stared at him, said,

'It's not soda.'

Ridge threw me a look of pure hatred. Malachy took the top off, downed a hearty swig, gasped as the raw alcohol bit and came as close to a smile as he ever would. A red flush already spreading across his mottled old face, he uttered,

'*Sin an fear.*'

Means 'that's my man', in total delight. Took another blast, blessed himself, said,

'Sweet Jesus, Mary and Joseph.'

No mention of the bollix who brought the stuff. We couldn't stay long as the doctors were doing their rounds and I didn't want to be there when they smelled the sheer potency of his breath. We had a lot of questions, but they could wait. Ridge gave him a gentle warm hug, lest she break one of those brittle bones.

I didn't . . . give him a hug.

The soda had definitely enlivened him and he spotted my hand, asked,

'What's with the glove? Some sort of Michael Jackson commemoration?'

I could have mentioned the item doing the rounds, Saint Pio's healing glove, but went mundane, said,

'Caught my fingers in a door.'

He stared at me, muttered,

'Drunk, no doubt.'

I fucking wish.

Ridge was silent and tight-lipped as we took the elevator down. She marched, and I mean marched, to the car, said,

'Get in.'

She had to be fucking kidding.

Right?

She, of all the people on the planet, knew how I responded to orders.

I asked,

'What's the bug up your arse?'

Not exactly PC, but then what was any more? Keys in her hand, she turned, venom jumping from her eyes, said,

'You brought spirits to a man just out of a coma?'

I tried for levity, said,

'Better than the usual – drink putting half the country into a coma.'

Didn't fly, oddly enough. She said,

'Every time I try to cut you some slack, you . . .'

She paused, fighting for some semblance of control, but losing, continued,

'And you just . . . just piss all over it.'

It was direct, I'll give her that. She indicated the car, and I said,

'Thanks, Officer, I'd prefer to walk.'

Was she finished?

Was she fuck.

Near screamed,

'I keep thinking you might change and then you descend to a new level of . . . of depravity.'

I began to walk away, said,

'Least I raised his spirits.'

I didn't look back, but the screech of tyres told me how she liked that.

The walk to town was treacherous, icy paths making a slip almost inevitable. An old woman ahead of me, walking as if her life depended on it (and it probably did), was making slow, uneasy progress. I was right behind her as she lost it, caught her just in time and managed to steady her.

She began to weep, said,

'I have to do the shopping, we haven't a thing in the house.'

I hailed a passing taxi. The driver rolled down the window, said,

'Taylor, I heard you were dead.'

I handed over some notes, said,

'Will you take this lady to the supermarket, wait for her and then bring her home?'

He shrugged, sure, no biggie.

I helped her into the back seat and she dried her eyes with a spotless white hanky, looked at me, said,

'You're an angel.'

The driver snorted.

I closed the door, nearly slipped doing it, and the cab eased away like a gentle ghost into the black city.

Not a story that I'd share with Ridge. She wouldn't believe it anyway. As I continued my careful walk, I thought,

'*What does that buy you?*'

And knew.

Nothing. Nothing at all.

Shops, buying used gold or laptops, musical instruments, DVDs, had sprung up almost overnight. They had fancy names but they were pawn shops, like the ones of my youth, where women pawned their husband's suit to put food on the table, and redeemed it if a wedding or funeral arose. Hoping for a funeral – mainly the husband's.

I stopped in the newest one in Mary Street, beside the vegetable outlet, and lo and wondrous, found the whole of the first season of *Breaking Bad*. For three euros and ninety-nine cents.

I was seriously delighted.

22

'Belief in nothing is at least a belief.'

Jack Taylor

I finally got to Garavan's in a little under an hour. All along
the route, I'd heard people bemoaning the

    burst pipes,

    homes without water,

    government threatening a water-rationing scheme.

Just deepened the gloom of a nation already despairing. I
stood at the counter, relishing the heat. The barman said,

''Tis like a biblical plague, wave after wave of chaos.'

He let my pint sit before he topped and creamed it off,
asked,

'Did you ever see the likes of it, Jack?'

No.

He handed me the *Irish Independent* and I took a corner
table. I was looking at all the sporting fixtures cancelled
when he brought over my pint and Jay outrider. I was working on the pint when a large, barrel-chested man
approached, sat down on the stool across from me. He had
a sparkling water with a slice of lemon, placed it neatly on
the table. I asked,

'Help you?'

He gave a bitter smile, said,

'I'm the new sheriff in town.'

I raised my pint, said,

'Good luck with that.'

Didn't faze him. He said,

'I'm a professional, a fully qualified investigator, so I'm here to tell you that you can officially retire.'

I took a swig of the Jameson, let it warm my gut, asked,

'Do I get a gold watch?'

He leaned across the table, said,

'Wise up, Taylor, you're done. The fucking state of you – hearing aid, limp, missing fingers, drinking before lunch. You're like a mangy alley cat, the nine lives fucked and gone, but no one told the poor bastard.'

I sat back, asked,

'You a Brit?'

Flash of anger, his fists actually bunched, he asked,

'What the fuck does that matter?'

I smiled, said,

'More than you think, Sheriff.'

He shook his head in disgust, said,

'I'm already on all the major cases in the city, so, Mister, don't let me find you staggering around in any of them. Do what you do best – drink yourself stupid.'

I let that hover, seep in, and asked,

'What about Headstone?'

'What?'

I leaned over to his face, said,

'Seems you missed one of the major cases. Not exactly a shining start to your professional career.'

He was mystified, said,

'Tell me about it.'

I said,

'The fucking dogs in the street know about it. Mind you, they are Irish dogs.'

He stood up, weighing the wisdom of walloping me in a pub where I was obviously a regular. Anger spitting from his eyes, he hissed,

'You've been warned, Taylor. Next time, I won't be so polite.'

I said,

'Be careful.'

He pulled himself up to his full height, looked at me, and I said,

'It's thin ice.'

He gave a short laugh, said,

'You think I'm worried by the bloody weather?'

I lifted my hands in mock surrender, said,

'Who's talking about the weather?'

He, dare I say it, stormed out.

Over the next couple of weeks, I continued to visit Malachy – without Ridge. One occasion, I left a carrier bag by the bed, containing a carton of cigs and the now customary bottle of 7Up. He eyed this, said with a twinkle in his eye,

'*Uisce beatha*, I presume?' ('The water of life.')

I said,

'It's certainly blessed to a lot of us.'

Saying thanks wasn't ever in the equation, but slowly, painstakingly, I managed to gather, in bits and scraps, his memory of the attack. I usually waited till he had a shot or four of the 7Up as that lessened the sheer terror in his eyes. I had no love for him, never had, but we had history – bad, yes, but still . . . I hated to see a defiant feisty spirit like his cowed.

He remembered.

Three young people, one a girl. The girl he regarded as being especially venomous. Said with a shudder as he clutched his bottle like a prayer he didn't believe in,

'She was on fire with pure hatred.'

'*Headstone*,' I thought.

Then I'd leave as his old head began to droop and sleep claimed him. A nurse stopped me one evening, said,

'You're a grand man to visit the priest like you do. You must love him very much.'

I had no reply to that. If she only knew.

She added,

'Is he related?'

Now I could answer, said,

'Only through drink.'

My black eye was now in the yellow phase, like having jaundice. I had tried so hard not to think of Loyola and his death in the cold water outside the cottage he loved and regarded as a refuge. Time to do something about it. I dressed to intimidate: black jeans, black T-shirt, heavy black scarf and my Garda coat. The Mossberg fitted snugly in the pocket. I took a Xanax, a wee drop of Jay, muttered, 'By all that's holy,' and went to the house previously occupied by Father Loyola. I didn't bring port. Knew the lady would be long gone.

Rang the bell, it was answered by a Barbie doll. Cross my heart, a real cutesy pie. Maybe twenty, not a day over. Jesus, at her age, I was security for a Thin Lizzy concert, a few years before Phil Lynott died.

She was heartaching gorgeous and, as if in deference, she wore a heavy silver cross round her neck. God forgive me, but all it served to do was accentuate her wondrous cleavage. Her clothes were the thin side of provocative. She asked, in a cultured voice tinged with the American twang beloved of Irish young people,

'Can I help you?'

Jesus, count the ways.

She clocked my hearing aid, my bruised eye, the glove on my right hand. Nothing there to suggest any help . . . could help. I said,

'I've an appointment with Father Gabriel.'

She chewed on her bottom lip and I knew if she had gum she'd probably have blown a bubble. I said,

'No need to show me the way.'

Pushed past her. I didn't knock on the door of the study, simply barged in. Gabriel was sitting behind a splendid new oak desk, a Galway Crystal tumbler of booze at his right hand. The walls were adorned with photos of him with the guys with the juice. Most of whom were now facing indictments for all sorts of fraud, embezzling, theft. I focused on the one with him and Clancy on the golf course, golden smiles and empty eyes. He managed,

'Jack, what a surprise. This is unexpected.'

I gave him my best smile. Even if my teeth had been real, the sentiment never would be. I sat in the armchair opposite him, lovely soft Napa leather that whispered, '*Relax.*'

He asked,

'To what do I owe the pleasure?'

I said,

'Give me a shot of whatever it is you're having.'

He had his control back, said,

'This is not really a good time.'

I said,

'Make it good.'

He glanced at the phone on his desk, one of those fake fucking antique jobs that cost a fortune, then decided to ride it out, reached in a drawer, produced a bottle of Laphroaig and a glass, poured a smallish measure, pushed it across the desk. I said,

'Ah, Johnny Depp's favourite drink.'

Contempt flowed easily now. He said,

'I really wouldn't know. Pop trivia is not my forte.'

I said,

'He's a movie star, but shite, that is one good drink.'

It was.

Like the smooth lie of an insincere priest. I said,

'Though is it not a bit unpatriotic of you not to support the home side, like a decent bottle of Jameson?

God knows, the economy could use all the help it can get.'

He was tired of me already, asked in a weary tone,

'Was there something?'

I made a show of looking around, asked,

'Where's the housekeeper?'

We both knew I didn't mean Barbie.

He made a dry sucking sound with his teeth, not an easy feat, but then, who'd want it to be? He said,

'Not really your concern, but she had divided loyalties.'

I pushed,

'Where is she now?'

Exasperation oozed from him. He took a fine nip of the fine booze, patriotism notwithstanding, said,

'I've absolutely no idea.'

And the sentinel riding point was,

'*And I couldn't give a fuck.*'

Reared in the school of not giving a fuck, I recognized a fellow pilgrim.

Time to up the ante, get him focused.

I stood up and he began to smile, thinking I was leaving. Used my left hand to free the Mossberg, pumped a shell into the chamber. The sound was awesome; you could have heard a nun drop. Momentarily startled, he managed to rein it in, said,

'Such theatrics, Taylor. You're going to shoot a priest?'

Now he laughed, at the sheer absurdity of the thought. The bollix hadn't been out much, it seemed. The laugh galvanized me, I was across the desk like I actually had the energy, the barrel jammed into his tanned cheek. I said,

'Great movie available on DVD, *Mesrine*, classic French cinema. In it, Mesrine says, "There are no rules, like me. I live without rules." You get my drift, I'd hazard. Here's the gig: you find the housekeeper and give her the money you "recovered" from poor old Loyola. Sound fair?'

He was shaken, it's hard not to be when a Mossberg is jammed into your face, but fair dues, he did rally, managed,

'Or what?'

I admire spirit, truly appreciate *cojones* in the face of a barrel, but, truth to tell, I didn't like this slimy bastard, simple as that.

I pulled the trigger an inch from his ear, blowing a hole in the wall almost the size of the Greek national deficit. Then the sound of running feet and the babe/housekeeper burst in. I said,

'Fuck off. And if I hear the phone, you'll be joining this dude.'

She took off.

I felt reasonably certain, not about to phone.

Gabriel, meanwhile, was whining,

'My ear, my ear, I can't hear.'

Fucking tell me about it.

I stepped back from the desk, adjusted my hearing aid, said,

'I can suggest a good ear man.'

He grabbed his glass, hands trembling, said,

'Taylor, you've no idea what you're getting into. The Brethren have a very severe code of punishment.'

I moved back to my seat, facing him, said,

'Like, say, drowning a helpless old man. Are you actually threatening me?'

The smirk was creeping back, not only on to his face but his very tone. He said,

'You can take it as a guarantee.'

He was either very drunk or very stupid. I grabbed the bottle, asked,

'May I?'

Even added a drop to his glass. I'm not vindictive . . . much. Asked,

'An actual threat from a man of the cloth, this is really something. You are serious, right?'

He lifted his glass, assured he'd regained the higher ground, back in control, the peasant in his place. I took a swig of the drink. It was smooth, smooth as false hope. I sat back, lit up a cigarette just to see the flicker of annoyance on his movie-star face, clicked the Zippo twice, asked,

'You hear that?'

He was all done with my idiocy, began to reach for a file, said,

'I can hear fine now . . .'

I held up my damaged hand, said,

'Sshhh.'

God forgive me, it's a rush to do that to a priest. They'd been trying for bloody centuries to keep us quiet, so throwing it back was a blast, if not indeed blasphemy. I put the Mossberg on the oak desk, would have loved it if he tried for it, reached in my jacket, took out a slim silver recorder. Bought it earlier in the day from the Army and Navy

shop. They even sold grenades, collectors' items. Asked,
'Ready?'

Hit the Play button.

His face took a serious drop as he heard his rich, clear
voice.

I let it play, then pressed Stop. Put it back in my jacket,
said,

'There will be two copies of this. One goes to Garda
headquarters in Dublin, unless your golfing buddy Clancy
really wants a copy? And the second to my friend
Kosta.'

He was speechless. Maybe he could join a Silent Disorder.

I continued,

'Kosta, I don't think you'd like much. He hates priests and
for some odd reason has a real hard on for you. He got me
the Mossberg and, cross my bedraggled heart, I love him
dearly but it has to be said, he's a nutter, your out-and-out
psycho. The, em, kind of guy who'd cut your balls off and
shove them in your mouth. Or so they say. I haven't actually
seen it but I think it's probably true. And here's the best bit.
You ready? He regards me as his great friend. Go figure,
huh? Anyway, sorry for rambling on like a priest on a
Sunday sermon, but the point is, if anything . . . *anything*
happens to me, if I were you I'd hope the Guards came
before Kosta. So you see, I don't like to be crude, but I have
you by the nuts.'

I stood up, drained my glass, put the gun back in my
jacket, said,

'Keep it in your pants, padre.'

The housekeeper was standing by the door, her face ablaze with anger and fury. She glared at me. I said,

'Alanna, I'm not the enemy. Your boss in there, he had the previous occupant of this house put in the river.'

She spat in my face.

I let the spittle dribble down my cheek, made no attempt to stop it, stared at her. She began to move back. I pulled off the glove, put my stumped fingers right in her face, lied,

'Your precious employer, the saintly Gabriel in there, he did that to me because he suspected I knew some things. I have one question for you.'

She was transfixed by the ugly remains of my hand, muttered,

'What?'

I pulled the glove back, asked,

'What does he think *you* know?'

23

'Don't play what's there, play what's not there.'

Miles Davis

The call from Kosta was unexpected. He began,

'Jack, you extended me the hospitality of your home. I'd like to repay the courtesy.'

It occurred to me that I knew next to nothing about him, and yet we had a deep, almost ferocious bond. I said,

'Of course.'

He gave me the address, in Taylor's Hill, our own upper-class part of the city, home to doctors and other professionals. He asked if I could be there by five and I said, sure. Then he added,

'I need your help, my friend.'

'You have it.'

A pause, then,

'Thank you. Please bring the Mossberg.'

Jesus.

Was I being invited to dinner or murder?

Taylor's Hill still retains those glorious houses set well back from the road, large, carefully tended gardens. Kosta's was midway, huge hedges almost shielding it, but you could glimpse the majesty of the building. Built when money was used lavishly on homes. I opened a heavy wrought-iron gate, and instantly two heavies were on me. Front and back. I said,

'Whoa, easy guys, I'm Taylor, and expected.'

The one facing me, all hard, mean muscle, gave me a cold, calculating look, then spoke into a lapel microphone, waited. Everybody wanted to be an FBI clone. He motioned,

'Pass.'

Not big on chat, those guys.

I moved up to the house, three storeys of Connemara granite kept scrupulously clean. I rang the bell and wondered if a maid would answer the door. Did people have them any more? Apart from the clergy, of course. Kosta answered. He was dressed in a navy-blue track suit not unlike Ridge's, trainers, a white towel round his neck. He greeted,

'Welcome to my home, Jack Taylor.'

Waved me in. A long hallway was lined with paintings. I know shite about art, but I do know about cash and here was serious dough in frames. The only painting I had was of Tad's Steak House in New York. He led me to a book-lined study. Not the books-for-show variety; you could see they'd been well used. Comfortable armchairs in front of a roaring log fire. Few things as reassuring as that. When I looked closer, I could see it was turf. A man who knew the country. He indicated for me to sit after I shucked off my coat. Left it close by. He offered a drink and I said,

'Whatever you're having yourself.'

'Gin and tonic?'

'Great.'

He didn't ask if I wanted it on the rocks. Serious drinkers don't do ice. I settled in the chair, putting the Mossberg on the carpet. Maybe he wanted it back.

He got my drink, and then he sat, reflecting for a moment as he gazed into the fire, the flames throwing what seemed close to a halo on to his bald skull. Like Michael Chiklis in *The Shield*. The Mossberg resting – a lethal snake – near his feet. He said,

'To good friends.'

'Amen.'

He liked that answer. Took a large wallop of his drink, savoured it, then swallowed, said,

'Genever.'

Dutch?

I've found nodding sagely stands you in good stead when you don't have a fucking clue.

I nodded sagely.

He let out a deep . . . Aah.

I knew we were now at the main event. He said,

'Jack, like you, I live my life to the minimum.'

He was kidding, right?

Bodyguards, a huge house . . . not really Zen. He continued,

'I have few friends, and you I regard as one. My history is violent but we don't need to dwell on that. I have one daughter, her name is Irini . . . means peace.'

Stopped.

Fuck, I hoped we weren't in sharing mode. No way was I reliving Serena May and that awful tragedy.

Pain ran across his eyes, took hold as he said,

'She is . . . otherworldly. Very beautiful, with a true purity of spirit. I have always, *siempre*, protected her.'

I believed him.

He said, slowly,

'But I was detained for nearly two years. She met a man named Edward Barton.'

He spat into the fire, continued,

'A Londoner. He smelled money, married her, and by the time I was . . . undetained, they had a daughter. This precious girl is five years of age now.'

Something had entered the room. Apart from the dark evening and the foul weather, there was a pervading sense of impending doom. Blame the Genever, I guess. Suddenly he was on his feet, grabbed a bottle, re-fuelled us. Then he put the bottle back, sat again, his body language reeking of rage. The line of his jaw was a study in controlled ferocity. He said,

'I despise this Edward. A low-life rodent, rank in every way. I put such shit under my heel every week, but Irini pleaded with me to be . . .'

Another pause as he searched for a word that wouldn't blow a hole through his face, said,

'Lenient. This man has spent all the money I had put aside for her. OK, I can deal with that. Money is not the issue. But then she comes to me, tells me this . . . man is . . . abusing their daughter.'

He let out a torrent of bile and obscenities that would have been impressive in their range if you weren't sitting a few feet from the source, realizing he was close to losing it. And with a loaded weapon at his feet, serious booze in his hand and system. You get the picture. He looked into the fire as a large piece of turf fell, and I'd swear I saw tears. A woman crying is always a man's undoing. But to see a man cry, fuck, especially a man like him, was a knife in the soul that would forever leave its imprint. I stayed with the sage gig, i.e., I said fuck all. He reined it in, took a deep breath, said,

'I am meeting this Edward soon – this evening. He needs more money. As he is not so stupid as to be unaware of my reputation, he insisted on a public place. Nimmo's Pier? You know it?'

Oh, shite, did I ever. Bad, bad history there.

He checked his watch, a slim Philippe Patek. I know of what I can never afford. He said,

'I'm to meet him in one hour.'

I knew where this was going so I volunteered for my own lynching, despite the fact that he had thugs in the garden and God knows where else. I said,

'Would you like me to come along?'

Fuck.

Fuck.

Fuck.

We both knew why I was there. He said,

'My regular employees – you met two on your arrival – are as loyal as money.'

I nodded, said with a sinking heart,

'Let's get this show on the road.'

We stood and he didn't thank me. If gratitude was a condition of our friendship, I wouldn't be there. He took me out to a large garage with a line of cars, selected a beat-up Volvo. Cops use them for one reason: to stay below the radar. Before he put the car in gear, he flipped the glove compartment open, expertly caught the Glock that tumbled out. He checked it was primed, said,

'Jack, my terrible dilemma is this: I can't harm the man. He knows that, my promise to my daughter, so he feels . . . invincible.'

We sat there as he waited for my answer, which could be nothing other than

'*I* haven't promised.'

He smiled, put the car in first, said,

'Exactly.'

We got there early, and to fill the time I told him about Father Gabriel and the drowning of Loyola. He produced a silver flask, drank from it and handed it to me. I didn't wipe the top, took a swig.

From where we were parked, we could see across the bay, the lights of Quay Street beckoning to come party. Kosta moved to get his back comfortable, said,

'One more thing, Jack. He has a driver, a new one, some Romanian trash named Caz.'

Oh, shite.

Christ on a bike, no. My decade-long sometimes friend.

He'd done the thing that counts in my narrow book: he'd come to see me in hospital – brought booze, too. In those ten years he'd been around a lot of, let's say, under-the-gun stuff I did. He worked with the Guards as a translator for the Romanian refugees, and not only could he have scored major brownie points with Clancy by selling me out, but got paid as well and secured his precarious position as a non-national. Superintendent Clancy was, yes, that keen to see me go down.

And, simply, deep down, I just liked him. Doesn't need any more analysis.

In one fluid movement, Kosta lit two cigarettes, handed one over. He had the instincts of a feral cat.

I took a drag, coughed. He said,

'Gitanes.'

Gypsies.

He was a veritable United Nations of moves, gestures and actions. And his instincts were uncanny. He said,

'Jack, your face tells me you know this man.'

When all else is up for grabs, sometimes the truth is the only way. I said,

'I do.'

He watched the ash on his cigarette, letting it build, then said,

'And he is a friend, *n'est-ce pas?*'

I considered, said,

'We're about to find out.'

24

'I cannot persuade myself that a beneficent and omnipotent God would have designedly created parasitic wasps with the express intention of their feeding within the living bodies of caterpillars.'

Charles Darwin

Bine was dressed in full combat gear, as if he was heading for a riot. All he needed was a face shield to complete the picture. Blown up behind, in glorious Technicolor, was the school. The relevant positions marked in red. He was wearing a holster holding a Walther, and around his neck hung beads with stones spelling out 'Medjugorje'.

Bethany watched him as he downed some speed, working up his shtick, getting ready to impress his minions. She thought, as she'd thought so many times, '*Arsehole*,' and wondered anew about men and guns. Like freaking kids with toys. Give them a weapon and even deadbeats like the lame brothers developed a swagger. Jesus, she wanted to puke. But she had a lust/heat gig going with Bine and still wasn't sure where it would go. Mainly, he gave her constant rage a focus. Gave her the jolt to feel alive. Also, she had to admit, when the sorry prick got ranting, he was mesmerizing. Got her to do stuff she'd never thought she'd have the grit even to attempt. And got her off on her little independent flights, like mind-fucking with the alcoholic

Taylor. Not something she felt it was wise to share with the crew.

And if they pulled it off – a first in Irish history, as Bine kept saying – she'd be famous. Maybe get on Oprah, have Angelina play her in the movie and be on the cover of *Hot Press*. One thing she knew: the girl rarely did jail time, she just did a Linda Kasabian and squealed. Even in the movies.

She tuned back in to Bine, took a hit of the speed her own self, washed it down with today's special, Jack Daniel's. Bine was into his rap. She'd missed the starters –   never mind, it wasn't too difficult to play catch-up. He said,

'Now this cat Stewart, the ex-dope-dealer, is a whole different ball game from the lesbian and Taylor. This dude has interests in the head shops, so that tells us the guy is clued in. He did six years in the Joy and no, I don't mean an English barmaid, I'm talking h-e-a-v-y time in Mountjoy. So the dude is cool, into some Zen bullshite, but real laid back and real sharp. I'm thinking, like, we got to waste the dude, right when we make our move, no bringing him back to base, just close his case there and then.'

He'd been ODing on *Pulp Fiction* again.

Bethany was dizzy trying to sort out his American expressions and distorted brain sequence. Bine looked at Jimmy, said,

'Your assignment is to watch this guy, 24/7. You hear what I'm saying? Like all the time, and when you get his routine down – and I mean like cold, bro – you report back.'

Jimmy was down all right, and nodding, not from the assignment but from the sheer amount of coke he had inhaled. His brother, always the sharper of the two, asked,

'Who's going to put out this dude's lights?'

Bine smiled, his recent tongue piercing still not healed, so his mouth looked like a sorry pit of disease, said,

'Eeny, meeny, miny, mo,

Catch a retard by the toe . . .'

His finger stopped at Bethany. He gave her that look that scared her, like he knew what she'd been thinking and was way ahead in the fuck-you department. He asked,

'You cool, babe? You up for this?'

She shrugged, said, 'Whatever,' getting enough boredom in there to convince him.

It seemed to. He asked,

'You gonna go up close and in the dude's face, like with the Stanley – or you wanna waste him mega, like with the AK?'

She risked a look into his eyes and just saw the psycho megalomania, said,

'I'm thinking the blade, yah know? Send a message to Taylor, let him know, like, it's on the edge, like we're burning bad.'

Even with drugs, sometimes she found it difficult to trot out the half-arsed Americanisms and ghetto gangsta shite. But he bought it, said,

'I'm liking it, lady. I'm real up on this.'

Bine downed his tumbler of Jack, gulped as it hit, turned to the blow-up of the school, and then, reaching for a Samurai sword – which were still legal to buy in Ireland – pointed out the entrance, said,

'I'm thinking, the bros go in here.'

Paused, did a little flick with the sword, nearly dropped it, which they'd have to pretend not to have seen, recovered, said,

'Here, the back, me and the babe, we'll do our mojo from here, start killing the retards as they head for the exit.'

He let that hover.

Jimmy asked,

'You got a head count in mind?'

Bine graced him with a bow, said,

'I'm thinking twenty-four would be, like, adequate.'

25

'Fever Kill.'

Tom Piccirilli

We got to Nimmo's ten minutes before the appointed time and in silence. Both of us thinking on Caz, but for wholly different reasons. Kosta, no doubt, wondering how much of a stand-up guy I was going to be. And me thinking how much of a friend do you have to be for me not to kill you?

A BMW, shining new, was already there, blocking the end of the pier. Kosta said,

'Ah. How predictable. He so likes his expensive toys.'

His eyes were aglow with such venom I could have lit a cig from them. He ordered,

'Reach in the bag for the satchel. The money is in that – the money he thinks is his.'

I gave it to him and he asked, without looking at me,

'Ready?'

'As rain.'

We got out, waited by the Volvo. The BMW bathed us in its lights. Two figures emerged, began to stroll towards us. Caz was nervous, I could see it in the slope of his shoulders.

And he didn't even know yet that I was part of the gig.

Edward.

Edward was glorious. Beautifully coiffed hair, blond, permanent tan, aviator shades, and, of course, of fucking course, an Armani suit.

Jesus, didn't anyone dress down any more?

He was striking in the way that sharks are. You could admire their sleekness but you didn't ever want to get close. He said,

'Who is this? I told you, Kosta, I told you to come alone.'

Now I could see Caz's nervous eyes and the twist in his body language. He was trying to say,

'No problem.'

Kosta said,

'My driver, like you have.'

Edward was enjoying the rush, the sense of calling the shots. He asked,

'Has he got a name?'

Kosta was totally relaxed, said,

'Employee.'

Edward enjoyed that a lot. Asked,

'You got my money?'

I kept hoping the macho posing, the cock-of-the-walk – or pier – bullshit would be all we'd have to deal with. These guys were having themselves a fine old time, strutting and mind-fucking. Kosta threw the satchel at his feet. Edward, without looking at Caz, said,

'Count it.'

As Caz knelt and began to do that, Kosta asked,

'How do I know this is the last time?'

Edward laughed, said,

'You don't know shit. I'll let you know when I'm done.'

Kosta looked at me and I slid the Mossberg out, racked the slide. Edward laughed harder, asked,

'Is that to scare me? Whoo-eh, I'm so afraid. Fuck your employee. Fuck you.'

I shot him in the face, range of about five yards.

The proximity nearly took his head off – clean off. Caz, on his knees, looked up as pieces of brain and gore splattered over the money and his face was a study in pure bewilderment. He began to rise when Kosta shot him between the eyes, a great shot if you weren't a friend of the one on the receiving end.

He moved fast, stood over Caz, put in the coup de grace. He glanced at me, the Mossberg still in position, and with his boot shoved Edward into the water. Then he turned, plucked the sodden notes from my dead friend's hand, pushed them in the satchel, said,

'You drive the Volvo, I'll follow in their car.'

A moment.

The gun in my hand, still hot from the firing, and I thought,

'*Yah think?*'

But Kosta was up and moving and I'd have to shoot him in the back.

He said,

'Jack, I'm truly sorry for your friend.'

I said,

'Not my friend any more.'

Lowered the Mossberg and got in the Volvo, reversed, turned towards the city, looked in my mirror to see Kosta boot my friend into the dark water. Said,

'*Codladh sámh duit, mo chara.*' Sleep safe, my friend.

Yeah.

I felt as fucking hollow as the words.

We got to Kosta's home and parked the cars. Standing outside, he touched my shoulder, said,

'Let's get inside, get some serious drink in us.'

I shrugged him off, said,

'Oh, I intend to get some serious drinking done, but not with you, not now.'

I began to walk down the driveway, knowing the thugs were at the gates in every sense, and my back was exposed to Kosta.

If he'd shot me, I felt he would have truly done me a service.

He didn't.

I made my slow way into town, got into a crowded Sheridan's on the docks, ordered a large Jay, took it outside so I could smoke and get wasted. As I was doing this a guy approached, started,

'Jack.'

Without looking, I said, 'Fuck off,' and looked across the

Claddagh basin to the pier. The double Jameson didn't erase what lay beneath the water. I don't think they've invented that drink yet, the one that wipes the slate of utter treachery.

26

*'Pick battles big enough to matter,
small enough to win.'*

Irish saying

The next week passed in a daze, Stewart and I trying to get a solid line on Headstone, both now feeling that time was of the utmost. That the major event these lunatics were planning was edging closer.

Friday morning, I was up early feeling numb, feeling dead. You kill an innocent friend, you get to hoping the fires of hell will be roasting. Dwell on it, and they already are. I had my coffee, black, bitter, strong, no sugar. No sweetness, Jesus, God forbid. Showered, shaved, Xanaxed to the goddamn hilt, switched on the radio.

Galway Bay FM. Jimmy Norman's breakfast show. Helped me chill. He plays the best music – music that makes you yearn. And he keeps it light, keeps it moving. He was saying that Keith (Finnegan) on the top of the hour had some special guests, but . . .

He had the Saw Doctors on the line from Australia.

Their manager, Ollie Jennings, is just about one of the nicest people I ever met.

And seeing as I don't do nice, that is unique. The Saw

Doctors, from Tuam, just down the road, were the perfect blend of traditional Irish and rock 'n' roll, and their own spin on live gigs had to be seen to be believed. They'd been around almost as long as I'd been slogging my befuddled gig in Galway. But they'd gone global. A new drummer, new album, and they sounded as down to earth as if they'd just released their first single. Not a notion in their repertoire. In America, when they'd said they were fans of Jodie Foster, she got in touch and, as the lads said, 'Went for a burger with them.'

I just loved that.

And, they said,

'She was quiet.'

There is something awesome in that apparently simple meeting. When a legend blends with the iconic and the result is humility, fuck, you want to shout,

'Bono, hope you're taking notes.'

Jimmy asked if they'd do a song, live, right then and there, and they did. Just sang.

My foot was tapping along, in the groove with the best of Irish, when the phone rang.

You get a call out of the proverbial blue that knocks the be-jaysus out of you. I'd had a dream on Thursday night that I still hadn't been able to shake. Laura was back in my life. I swear, I could feel her hand in mine.

For reasons not at all.

We were feeding the swans at the Claddagh, and she leaned back into my shoulder and I was so deliriously happy.

And woke.

Tears on my face, coursing down my cheeks.

Hard arse that.

Had muttered, in a vain attempt to shake it away,

''Tis the holy all of it.'

The awful loss had paralysed me. I'd sat on the side of my empty bed, woebegone, in fucking bits, then shouted,

'Get a fucking grip.'

Had.

Kind of.

I'd made my own self busy, and then pulled on a sweat-shirt that bore the logo: *NUIG, Ropes.*

My oldest 501s and my winter crocs, the ones that whispered,

'We love you, love your feet.'

You are getting love from shoes, you are so seriously deranged, it's pathetic.

And I'd been relishing Jimmy's show with the Saw Doctors, hated having to answer the damn phone. Said,

'Yeah.'

In that icy tone.

'Mr Taylor, it's Sister Maeve.'

I had given her my number, never, never expecting to hear from her. But nuns, they give nothing away, in every sense. I said,

'Ah, good morning, Sister.'

Lame, right?

She replied,

'Mr Taylor, you are a very unusual man, a mix of tremendous sadness and such violent acts.'

I'd need a little more to go on than my character analysis, said,

'I'll need a little more to go on.'

I swear to God, she seemed to be suppressing utter joy, said,

'Father Gabriel and his . . . housekeeper have taken off with all of the Brethren's funds.'

Gabe did a runner? I knew I'd got his attention, but that he legged it, phew-oh. I was literally lost for words, tried,

'Really?'

Now she let it loose, said,

'Oh, Mr Taylor, it means the Brethren are a spent force. Their terrible shadow has been lifted.'

I said,

'That's great.'

Meant it.

She replied with,

'Mr Taylor, I've become familiar with your methods and I don't much approve, but this . . . I knew you were involved and you turned it around, did our Church a true service. God bless you, Jack.'

And rang off.

I was still trying to digest this when my mobile shrilled.

Stewart.

'Jack, starting today, I'm going to be at my head shop every day at three. I've let my routine out along the grapevine so people know where they can find me. If you're right and they're trying to make a move on me, well, now they'll know how.'

I said,

'Give it three, four days, they'll bite.'

'What makes you so sure?'

I thought about all we'd discussed, tried to figure it out, said,

'They are working towards a very definite timetable and everything needs to be in place for the mad bastards.'

He gave that some thought, then said,

'Why are you so certain they'll target me?'

Easy answer if not exactly true.

'You got a headstone in the mail, as did Ridge and I. We have both been . . . shall we say . . . contacted.'

He sounded just that little bit wary – not a trait he displayed much – asked,

'You'll have my back, right?'

'Count on it, buddy.'

He lingered, reluctant to ring off, said,

'Three to four days, you think?'

'Absolutely.'

For the first time in my chaos-ridden life, I'd called it right on the money.

Like a Galway snapshot of a particular era, I was staring out at the lone Galway hooker, at easy anchor in the bay. No, not a working girl, a beautiful boat built in Galway. It gave me a vague comfort that is inexplicable. I'd taken a moment to go down to the docks and just stare at it, knowing this might well be the last visual peace I'd have. Then turned to the city and the business of bait.

As we waited for Stewart to establish his routine, I went to the city centre each day, never knowing how some chance encounter might yield information. I nearly looked for Caz, had to switch channels, focus on the job at hand. Had an encounter all right, just not one of any normality.

I was limping along Shop Street, trying to avoid all the buskers; you give to one, you better give to all. A man stopped me. I vaguely remembered him from way back, when I had a career and he had notions. Not either of us, not any more. Life had wiped the slate clean. Dave. I don't know how I dragged up his name, but he'd been a player in the property game. Rode it till the bust and then went belly up himself. I'd always kind of liked him as beneath his posing I'd detected a deep hurt from childhood – the industrial schools that only Seamus Smyth has ever really captured on paper; concentration camps for young boys, militarized by the Church. He tended to talk in sound bites, lest you ever nail him down. He launched,

'Jack, the cuntin' bank refused my plea for an extension of my mortgage.'

You'd infer from this that I saw him regularly, was intimate with his life. Such are the Irish, tell you all or fuck all. I hadn't laid an eye on him for over ten years. He'd weathered that decade badly, if appearances were any indication. Shabby clothes, furtive eyes, a face of broken veins and that purple complexion of the desperate drinker.

He continued,

'I'm going to lose my house, and what am I going to tell my daughters? The youngest is only eleven.'

I wanted to scream,

'The banks will lend you millions, but crush you if you owe a paltry sum.'

But asked,

'How much to buy you some time?'

His eyes nearly rolled in his head. If not salvation, at least a lifeline. He considered, then gave a figure. Not the amount he wanted to give, but he knew me well enough not to act the bollix.

I could just about manage that, from Father Gabriel's blood money. I said,

'Meet me in the Quays tomorrow at twelve. I'll have it in cash for you.'

He was stunned, said,

'You're a good man, Jack.'

My dad was a good man.

I wasn't.

And you've got to think,

'The fuck was with that?'

Trying to buy redemption with one measly act of generosity?

I don't know, maybe.

The next day, I delivered the money as promised. After, did I feel better?

Did I fuck.

I was torn apart by fresh dreams of Laura and the sheer loss of her. A shrink told me one time when I was in the home for the bewildered and the confused, the loony bin,

'Jack, it's not that you're afraid to be happy, but that you're terrified of making someone else unhappy.'

I stopped at Wolfe Tone Bridge, the city swirling around me, my heart in scorched ribbons, tears trying to make inroads on my beaten face. Then got a grip, sort of, muttered,

'A pint and chaser mightn't help, but, sure as rain, might bring oblivion.'

I turned towards Neachtain's, not a pub I used much as it was so busy, but now I needed the sound of people. The sheer volume of a thousand stories that had no bearing on my life, just to drown in the variations.

Buttoned my all-weather coat, my act in gear, if not really in place.

27

'The sad line of slow suicides.'

Jack Taylor, watching a batch of huddled drinkers

There weren't a whole lot of things, then, to make you smile, but I was flicking through the *Irish Daily Mail*, came across a cartoon by the gifted Graeme Keyes. Showed a full shot of The Sanctuary at Knock. The Irish answer to Lourdes.

A bewildered pilgrim, with rosary beads around her neck, staring at a signpost which read

> To Knock
> To Mass
> To Mass Hysteria

And in the corner, an excited pilgrim gasping,
'The sun actually danced.'
Facing him is a less exalted pilgrim who sighs,
'Wow, the sun actually appeared.'
Classic. Summed up the whole nation.
I was waiting for Stewart. He'd arranged to come to my apartment and I'd mocked,
'Bring your own herbal tea.'

He did.

He arrived at noon as the Angelus bell rang. I was probably one of the three remaining people in the country who still said the prayer.

Stewart brought herbal tea, a box of McCambridge's cookies and an attitude.

None of which I welcomed.

I pointed at the kettle, said,

'Knock yourself out.'

No disrespect to the aforementioned shrine. He made the tea, placed the cookies on a plate, I kid thee fucking not. A plate? Said, with gusto,

'Join me.'

Right.

I got a bottle of Blue Moon from the fridge, joined him at the table and dared him to comment. His eyes were fixated on the gun.

'Is that a Mossberg?'

I was impressed, said so, added,

'Modified to fit in my jacket.'

He had an avalanche of comments, reined them in, bit down on a cookie, then noticed my glove. I got there first, said,

'Keeps me from freaking out.'

He drank his tea, seemed to enjoy it, then said,

'The attacks on the vulnerable are continuing. The Guards insist they are isolated incidents and not connected.'

Looked right at me, asked,

'Are you familiar with Darwin?'

I flexed my non-existent fingers, tried,

'*Origin of Species*. I'm waiting for the movie.'

He ignored that, said,

'Certain things Darwin wrote and said have been used and subverted – let's say, reinterpreted – to fit the delusions of various whack jobs.'

I waited while he took out a notebook, read a piece and asked,

'Know who wrote that interpretation?'

I said,

'No.'

He was all focus now, said,

'Columbine, the two high-school killers.'

The light bulb nearly exploded over my head as I realized.

'Columbine. The fucker who took my fingers – they called him Bine.'

And the awful understanding then of what my mind had been edging about. I said,

'Jesus, they're going to hit a school – be the first Irish event.'

He nodded, could see I was coming fast up to speed. Christ, I needed to chill. Went to the bedroom, drew down two Xanax from my stash. Dry swallowed them, my mind ablaze. I came back to Stewart, who was about to say something, but I cut him off with,

'Drink more tea, let me think. Don't talk, do some Zen shite or something.'

He did. Leaned back in the chair, curled his body up into a ball of relaxation, closed his eyes, went . . . away.

I scanned the notes I'd made, let all the data saturate, pumped the Mossberg to keep me hyped, then after fifteen, twenty minutes, I said,

'Stewart, they're going to hit a special needs school.'

He was appalled, hadn't got that far in his own musings, asked,

'What are we going to do?'

I knew, beyond a shadow, said,

'Keep with the bait gig.'

Course, he had to ask, sooner or later, ever since I'd suggested he establish a routine,

'You think of me as bait?'

Had to defuse it a bit.

'Truth to tell, I rarely think of you at all.'

To soften it, I added,

'I'll be there in the shadows, and if . . . if we can just grab one of the bastards . . .'

My track record of reliability was not a great recommendation, and I could see that flit across his face. He had to ask,

'What if you're not . . . not able to intervene effectively?'

I told the truth, said,

'Then you're seriously fucked.'

When he was leaving, he admitted,

'I'm a little spooked, Jack.'

I lied, said,

'Spooked is good, keeps you alert.'

I sat on the sofa, drenching myself in all that had happened, thought, a Judas goat? Is that what I was doing to Stewart?

Fucked if I could deny it.

Then told myself, I'd better get in the routine my own self. Start shadowing Stewart as I'd promised.

I got my coat and the Mossberg, and headed out.

Checked my watch. Stewart wouldn't be at the head shop yet, so I figured on a fast pint.

No.

I owed it to him to at least appear to hold it together, so I went to the tiny café at the bottom of Quay Street. It was quiet and I ordered a double espresso. Was on the first sip when a stunning woman came in, looked round and caught me looking at her. She walked over, asked,

'Mr Taylor?'

'Jack, but yes.'

'May I sit?'

Was she kidding? She could sit for ever and I wouldn't stir. The truly beautiful are almost painful to see. You know that such a gift has to bring a price of some kind, if only age alone. Sure enough, she seemed to have an aura of sadness. She had that French elegance: effortless, compelling and utterly fascinating. And she knew it and was not at ease with the knowledge. Before I could catch my breath or offer a coffee, she said,

'I'm Irini.'

And I knew, deep down, with a sense of dread, that this was not going to make me feel good. I said,

'Kosta.'

She nodded and began to speak.

One meeting, can it change your life? Maybe. It can certainly twist and change your whole previous way of thinking.

When she left, I knew what I'd have to do and hated it. No ducking this bullet. It had my name on it, in neon.

Stewart and I had met again after the first day of his routine began, going over our respective roles and what would go down after – if there was an after. Finally, when all had been gone over so many times, he reached in his jacket and handed me over a syringe. I said,

'You think we need this?'

He was edgy, snapped,

'You'll need it. This is your half-arsed plan.'

I took it and was about to inquire what it contained but he was way ahead, said,

'You don't want to know. Try to jab it in the neck. Works faster and I'm thinking we won't have a whole lot of time.'

I'd set up my kitchen in the optimistic hope that we could actually grab one of them and haul their crazy body back here.

Day four, I was beginning to think I was as nuts as Stewart implied. Standing across the street from the head shop, the syringe in my right pocket, way back in the shadow of a doorway and forcing the talk with Irini out of my mind, I nearly missed the movement.

Then –

Jesus, the girl, Bethany, setting up camp in the alley next

to the shop. I fumbled for my mobile, got Stewart, rushed,

'She's here, right next to you.'

A sharp intake of breath from him, neither of us really prepared for my prediction working. I added, trying to keep the panic at least one sentence away,

'Come out of the shop real fast, don't give her time to think about it, cross the street. When you get to your car, drop your keys and bend down to retrieve them.'

He said,

'Jack, you ready for this? You really don't want to fuck this up. Tell me you know what you're doing.'

I clicked off.

Best to keep him on high alert.

A minute later, he emerged, looking for all the world like a young harassed entrepreneur, and did exactly as I said. Nearly got run over as he pushed across the street.

It worked, took her by complete surprise, but she rallied.

Went after him.

I moved.

She was looming over the bending Stewart when I hit her with the needle. She never sensed me, so sure was she of her prey. I plunged the needle into her jugular, slapped the Stanley knife easily from her hand, grabbed her as she began to crumple, pulled open the back door, shoved her in. Stewart was right: that concoction was fast. I could hear a slight whimper from her. Now, the rough part. Stewart was in the driver's seat. I took a deep breath, leaned against the door, nonchalance personified, lit a cig, scanned the area and saw nothing, and heavens blessed, no sirens. My nerves only evident in the flicking of the Zippo.

I knew Stewart was going crazy and to see me leaning against the car must have upped his anxiety to a whole new level. I risked a glance into the back seat. She was out.

Phew-oh.

I stubbed the cig under my boot, casually slid into the shotgun seat. Stewart was shaking, and, as I watched, he reached in his pocket, took out a pill, swallowed it. I said,

'Thought you didn't take dope.'

He waited as he let the pill slide down, said,

'Thought I didn't abduct people either.'

He let out a breath, put the car in gear, said,

'Your apartment, right?'

I nodded and we got out of there.

Our insane luck held and we got to the apartment without any screams of outrage or attention. Carried the girl to the apartment. Inside, we faced the hard kitchen chair, under-lined with tarpaulin. For show, on the counter, were a range of what looked like surgical instruments, gleaming like terror. If she was like most young people, she'd have seen:

Saw

Hostel

The Ring

and all the other gruesome torture flicks doing the biz. Her imagination would do the rest.

Convinced Stewart, who croaked,

'You're not seriously going to use . . . those?'

I didn't look at him, said,

'I seriously don't know.'

We put her in the chair and I produced the rope. Stewart went pale, said,

'Jesus, Jack, are we going too far?'

I lost it, ranted,

'*We?* The fuck is the *We* shite? You're going to fuck off for an hour, have some Zen time, and when you return, I'll have the answers.'

He left reluctantly, reiterating,

'One hour?'

'Yeah, fucking time me if you like.'

Slammed the door.

Maybe that, or the drug wearing off, but I heard Bethany stir. I turned back into the apartment.

The next hour is not something I want to think about, ever. Two voices running rabid in my head. The first:

'*Torturing and psychologically destroying a young girl. Is this what you've slithered your way down to?*'

The second:

'*The Devil drives.*'

I clung to this as it elaborated,

'*She is a stone killer. Preys on the weak and vulnerable and is about to go after a special needs school.*'

Her eyes widened as I approached and she spat,

'Taylor.'

I held up my mutilated hand, said,

'Now you get a choice. Tell me what I want to know without any incentives . . .'

Threw a glance at the ugly shining instruments, as she did, continued,

'Or we can do it your way. Sorry I don't have a headstone, but you'll find it's memorable anyway and, trust me, you'll talk, so why not spare us both the grief?'

I moved back as she roared,

'Fuck you, alky!'

I took the other kitchen chair, sat cowboy style, my arms resting on the back. She looked at the bindings, spat,

'Into bondage, is that it?'

I said,

'You wanted Stewart, he'll be back soon.'

She took a fast look at my hand, said,

'Could almost pass for normal. Almost.'

I rose from the chair, took out a bottle of Jameson, poured a measure, knocked it back, asked,

'Thirsty?'

Her eyes pleaded yes but her body held fast. I pushed,

'Why did you pose as Ronan Wall's sister?'

A snicker, then,

'You dumb arse, he's my lover.'

I smiled and she instantly realized her error. I said,

'So now we have one name. Just yours and the other two losers to go. Oh, and the special needs school. I'll need to know where and when.'

Her eyes darted around. Being alone with me was not giving her much confidence but she tried,

'What are you going to do, kill me? You haven't the balls for that.'

She was right and I was having serious reservations about being able to do this. Truth is, she looked kind of pathetic and vulnerable. But by pure awful chance, the sun chose that exact moment to send a brief ray of light through my kitchen window and it hit on a gold pendant around her neck. Just a glimpse of it, but it shone. Oh Jesus, did it ever. The Claddagh jewellery I'd bought for Laura. She was wearing it.

Rage engulfed me. I snapped it from her neck and she laughed, said,

'Oh, was that for your American floozy?'

My Walther PPK was in her purse. I gritted my teeth, asked,

'Where is the Medjugorje relic I was wearing?'

She smiled, said,

'We threw it in the trash. We don't believe in all that bull-shit religious mumbo-jumbo.'

I stood, trying to control the ferocious violence her words aroused in me. Said,

'Believe this.'

I moved to the fridge, took out a bottle of water, asked,

'Is sparkling OK?'

We were done a good ten minutes before Stewart returned. I'd released her from her bonds, led her to an armchair where she curled up in the foetal position, whimpering like a savaged puppy. There wasn't a mark on her.

That you could see.

She was, in Irish,

'*Briste.*' Broken.

I put a mug of Jameson in her hand. She needed both hands to hold it, then gulped it down lest I withdraw it. She wouldn't meet my eyes.

Thank Christ.

Back in my early days, I was assigned to the Border. One wet dark Friday, Stapleton and I were sent to Belfast, a few weeks before Bloody Sunday. Told,

'Keep your mouths shut, the sound of your brogues would have the UVF all over ye.'

Civilian clothes, of course. We had no idea why we were going and to this day, I'm sure the ones who sent us hadn't a clue either. Those days, it was retaliation and madness. Still is, but with a political sheen to gloss over the uglier aspects.

Saturday night, we were taken to a dank, dark basement on the outskirts of the city. No idea if we were the ones who might be sacrificed. No one knew anything then, save it was possible the next atrocity was you. We were being taught a lesson. Here's how it went down.

A cocky, confused lieutenant from the Paras First Brigade was tied to a chair, not a whole lot unlike the one in my kitchen. He was mocking his captors, going,

'Thick as planks, fucking Paddies.'

You had to admire his spunk, if not his intuition. The men in that room, silent as mourners, had seen and done things that no man should ever witness. You wanted to scream at the mad bastard in the chair, '*Look, look at the men you're throwing insults at.*'

Their eyes had that granite, dead expression of '*We've been to hell and we've brought it back.*'

And still the Para continued to lash them with insults about Fenian bastards, Papist morons.

The unit leader said to me,

'See that snooty bollix? He's trained to withstand anything. And the stupid fooker believes his training will help him.'

He was chugging from a silver flask, handed it to me, grimacing as he swallowed his. I drank, near choked, but managed to hide it, and he said,

'The holy trinity: coffee, *poitín* and Guinness.'

Lethal.

He asked,

'Got a watch?'

'Sure.'

'Look at it.'

I did.

He said,

'Fifty minutes is my record. I've bet the boyos I can get it down to forty-five minutes or all drinks on me tonight.'

He did.

The water gig was only part of it. The Para was freed from his restraints, covered in faeces, urine, vomit and shame. He fell on the floor among the remnants of his once fine teeth, scattered on the wood like bloody nuggets of careless cruelty. He begged,

'Shoot me.'

We were then hustled out, fast, to a shebeen, the illegal

drinking clubs of the Movement. Had us one hell of a night, céilidh music and the rousing songs:

'The Men Behind The Wire'
'James Connolly'
'The Girl From The County Down'.

None of it could erase the sound I'd heard as we reached the top step of the basement, on our way out.

A single shot.

28

'You can't take down a headstone.'

Fervent belief in the west of Ireland

December 8th.

I checked the calendar, saw it was Our Lady of the Immaculate Conception's Feast Day, and hoped to God she might lend a hand. Just in case, I doubled up on the Xanax. Two more in my all-weather Garda coat, nestling beside the Mossberg. A silver flask given to me by Laura, jacked with Jameson, and a crushed-to-powder amphetamine. Bring me up to speed, so to pun. My heart was racing and my hands had a slight tremor.

Fuck.

With the cocktail of stuff I had in my system, I'd either

Die

Throw up

Or settle.

My stomach was losing the plot, didn't know did I want to be cranked, mellow, on fire or what the blazes. The Xanax won out. Thank Christ. The questions that had been plaguing me: Will Bethany tell? Will they be waiting in ambush for us? The pills whispered,

'*Chill.*'

I did.

Left the apartment, a freaking one-man army of pharmaceuticals and firepower. A half-arsed version of the American Dream. In my mind were uncoiling the words of 'Dixie'. Elvis hadn't so much left the building as stormed out with murder aforethought.

Limped across the Salmon Weir Bridge.

Cut by the Town Hall, announcing a forthcoming Marc Roberts evening. I'd go if I was still mobile. Then into Wood Quay, turned into Eyre Square. Paused.

Might be the last time I'd see it. The Xanax said,

'*Fuck it, you've seen it enough, drive on.*'

I did.

Threw a glance at Debenhams, soon to lay off ninety per cent of the staff. Jesus. Came to the Meyrick Hotel and turned into Forster Street. About one hundred yards now from the designated killing zone.

My heartbeat had settled as I walked into the car park behind the school. I could hear the kids, the delighted shrieks of joy and childhood. As I found a place to crouch, hidden behind two cars, another school bus arrived, dispatching some of the special needs children. Most seemed to be Down syndrome. Tore and ripped at my shredded heart. I bit down, made her face go away. My mobile shrilled, putting the heart sideways in me. Answered.

Stewart.

He was parked outside the school, where Bethany had divulged the two brothers would launch. He asked,

'You . . . OK, Jack?'

'Yeah, you?'

Pause, then,

'Nervous and alight with adrenaline.'

I said, 'Hush,' seeing a white van turn into the car park. Exactly as Bethany had told me. Crossed my mind to shout, like Sam Shepard in *Black Hawk Down*, 'Abort, abort, abort.' I whispered,

'They're here, *bí cúramach.*' (Be careful.)

He took the deepest breath I'd ever heard, replied,

'*Leat féin.*' (You too.)

Clicked off.

Lock and load.

The van opened, four figures spilled out, all dressed in black combat gear, and on the back of the jackets, in red . . . HEADSTONE. I thought, fucking everybody advertises. A large combat bag was on the ground and they began to pull out its contents.

A fuckin' arsenal. Enough firepower to keep Afghanistan lethal for a year. The two brothers, with Remington rifles and grenades, ran to the front of the building.

The remaining two:

Bethany, appearing strung out and spaced, held a shotgun in her thin arms.

Then Bine . . .

Fuck, I recognized him. Ronan Wall, the swan killer, the psycho brat, shielded by money and upbringing, to get to this – a massacre of handicapped kids?

Like fuck.

He was barking at Bethany and I felt a twinge of sorrow for her. She hadn't told, had shown up, knowing we'd be waiting, and had that awful expression of the truly doomed, nigh pleading,

'*Do it.*'

Mr Macho, having torn her a new arsehole, began to arm up. A bandolero of shells around his shoulder, a Glock in his hip holster and the *pièce de résistance*, the Remington Pump, in the neighbourhood of my Mossberg, but not as rapid. The guy loved hardware. Starring in his own movie, he racked the pump, pushing shells into the chamber like a good 'un. I was about to send his movie straight to video. He slammed the van door, then marched towards the school's back door. I stepped out, said,

'Hi, buddy.'

He turned around, stunned. His mind couldn't quite collate the scenario. He said,

'Fucking Taylor, always fucking Taylor. The fuck is with you, man, following me around?'

I said,

'I like swans.'

As they say in literary novels, a frozen tableau. The tableau gives that careless hint of learning without pushing it. Ronan finally got it, turned to Bethany, said,

'You cunt.'

Shot her twice in the face. I clubbed him with the Mossberg and he went down fast – not out, but dazed. I moved to Bethany, cradled her head in my arms for a moment, tried not to look at her devastated face, muttered,

'Thank you.'

If she heard me, she gave no sign, just a soft sigh as she let go of all the troubled existence of her short life. I felt a torrent of rage escape as I turned back to Bine/Wall/the fuck ever. He was reaching for the Glock on his hip. I kicked it effortlessly away, pushed his legs apart, stood over him, the Mossberg pointed at his groin, reached down, pulled his top aside, and tore my Medjugorje chain from his neck. He said, spitting blood and teeth from where I'd clubbed him,

'What now, Taylor? You going to shoot me?'

He gave a harsh laugh, pushed his hand towards me, commanded,

'Help me up.'

I put my mutilated hand in his face, said,

'Alas . . .'

Added,

'All I can give you is . . . the index finger.'

I looked down at the concrete he was lying on, said,

'See that slab you're on? Kind of like a headstone, you think?'

He spat in my face, said,

'Get real, Taylor. I'm connected. Like, I got juice. So fold your pathetic tent and fuck off. I have history to write.'

I gut-shot him.

Let him savour that awhile. Moved the barrel up to his right eye, the one the swans hadn't taken all those years ago, asked,

'This your good eye?'

He was finally beginning to realize that maybe there was a court of no appeal, that no family, money, upbringing, class, would step in to save him. He pleaded,

'I'm insane, don't know what's right or wrong, you have to get help for me. Right, Jack?'

I said,

'The thing with your good eye is, you'll see it coming.'

He did.

I pumped three shells in there and kicked his fucked-up body for good measure.

Then I was moving as if the Hound of Heaven was nipping at my heels, thinking,

'*We get out of this, I might even go back to Mass.*'

Heard the wail of sirens, a whole shitload of them. Kept moving. I was near the end of Forster Street when Stewart pulled over, the door open, the engine still primed. He screamed,

'Move. Fast.'

I did.

Sweat teeming down my cheeks, I glanced at Stewart. He wasn't much better. We were past the Meyrick Hotel, turning down by the tourist office and into Merchant's Road. Stewart not booting it, but desperately wanting to.

Tick.

Tick.

Tick.

I could hear the clock, not on our side. One error and we were fucked. Outside McDonagh's, but a docker from the

water, he pulled into a vacant space near the hardware store.
I opened the flask, took a deep hit, offered it. He took it,
coughed, near spluttered, gasped,

'The fuck is that?'

I said,

'My own concoction. I might patent it, call it Headstone.'

He wasn't amused but did take another hit. I was finger-
ing the Medjugorje stones like an unreasonable mantra. He
asked,

'What's that?'

I said,

'A hint of grace.'

We tried to get our respective shredded nerves in gear.

I asked,

'How'd the Guards respond so quick?'

He stared straight ahead, said,

'I called them.'

Jesus wept.

I grabbed the flask back, hit it with ferocity, said,

'Fucking great, just brilliant, Christ Almighty.'

He continued,

'Actually, I called Ridge, said she'd find two wannabe
Columbines handcuffed to the front door. And that two
more shooters were at the rear, so to bring back-up. The
credit and publicity will rocket her career.'

I said nothing, so he asked,

'How'd it go for you?'

Almost dreading the answer, he knew it wasn't going to be
good. I sighed, said,

'A lover's quarrel. Bine/Ronan Wall, he shot her after she opened up on him with her Walther.'

An indication of how madness, gunplay, adrenaline affect people, he asked the most inane question:

'She had a Walther?'

'She does now.'

Part of him wanted the details, but most of him didn't, so he went with,

'And you think the Guards are going to buy that?'

I nodded.

'Sure, wraps it up nice and tidy.'

The booze had calmed him. He leaned back, his head on the seat, then said,

'OK, you think if we get past this, you might really tell me how it went down?'

I considered for all of two seconds, said,

'I seriously doubt it.'

Ridge was on the front page of all the newspapers, banners proclaiming:

Hero Ban Garda prevents first Irish Columbine.

The accounts reported that she overpowered the two brothers but, despite her valiant efforts, was unable to prevent the deaths of the ringleaders, who apparently had, in a bizarre pact, killed each other. Sales of *We Need to Talk About Kevin* went through the roof. Gus Van Sant's *Elephant* and Michael Moore's *Bowling for*

Columbine sold out of HMV and Zhivago.

The papers speculated on the weird deaths of Bethany and Wall and concluded:

A love affair, fuelled on drugs and would-be celebrity, gone berserk when faced with the enormity of what they were about to undertake.

Yada fucking yada, on they went, fuel for the talking heads. Most of the editorials called for Ridge to receive the President's Medal of Honour. Promotion was a given.

She called me, demanded,

'We have to talk.'

'I don't think so.'

A pause, then,

'Jack, I can't accept credit for what I didn't do.'

Jack!

I weighed my words, let loose,

'Stewart gave you shelter when you needed it. You open this can of worms, he might go to jail. Trust me on this, he would not be able to do time again.'

Slam dunk.

I hoped.

Then,

'Jack, I need you to tell me the truth about something.'

'Fire away.'

Tentative,

'Did you have anything to do with the deaths of the girl and Ronan Wall?'

I could see Al Pacino in *The Godfather II* as Diane Keaton asked him something similar, said,

'You get to ask me this just one time, right?'

'OK.'

'No.'

Did she believe me?

Did she fuck.

I could feel the cluster of questions she had but she let them slide, said,

'So I'm indebted to Stewart, then.'

'More than you know.'

'Jack . . . *Bí cúramach* . . . be careful.'

'*Leat féin* . . . you too.'

I had two calls to make. Rang Directory Inquiries and got the number of the new private investigator in town, Mr Mason. Rang and he answered with,

'Ultimate Investigations Inc.'

I said,

'I've heard you are a great PI.'

Let him bask.

He did.

Then he said,

'Well, thank you, we do our best, or as our slogan says, our Ultimate.'

Jesus.

I said,

'I've some hot information for you.'

'Your name, please?'

'David Goodis.'

He was all biz now, barked,

'So David, let's hear it.'

I gave him Kosta's address, said he was about to move a major mountain of coke at seven that evening, but to be careful, he always carried a Glock and was extremely dangerous. He was involved in the killing of that Ronan Wall. Rang off before he could quiz me.

Then called Kosta. Opened with,

'It's Jack.'

He didn't sound surprised. If anything, he was friendly, said,

'Thanks for returning my car.'

I launched,

'You helped me in so many ways so, to clean the slate, I wanted to warn you that a guy posing as a PI is going to arrive at your home at seven o'clock. He's been hired by the Romanians to avenge Caz's death. I don't know how they manage to get their information, but they do. Maybe the daily threat of deportation has them on constant alert.'

He digested this, then said,

'Thanks, Jack. Maybe after this . . . matter, we can be friends again?'

I let that dance, said,

'We'll always be close.'

He laughed, said,

'A bottle of Stoli is waiting in the ice bucket, my friend.'

On ice.

I said,

'Works for me, *hermano.*'
He finished with,
'*Del corazón, mi amigo.*'

29

'There is no such thing as a clean kill.'

Gypsy proverb

Kosta phoned the following evening, just after the Angelus bell had tolled. Outside a fierce storm was blowing. One of those sudden blasts of terror that comes without warning. The windows in the apartment shook from the power of it. He said,

'Yesterday evening was as you had forewarned me, thank you.'

I already knew how it went down. Had called the Guards' hotline and told them a crazy man was going to try and trespass on Kosta's property. They were waiting for him and he was now in custody, trying to Brit his way out of a gun charge and various other violations.

'You all right?'

He laughed, said,

'I am, but my visitor – let's say he won't be making house calls for a time. The police were not exactly gentle in their handling of him.'

As if it had just occurred to me, I said,

'Come pick me up, we'll celebrate.'

Now a trace of caution entered his voice.

'Jack, it's blowing up a hurricane now.'

I laughed.

'It's Galway. If you let the weather dictate your life, you'd never go out.'

His intuition battled with his machismo and he conceded, said,

'OK, I'll see you in twenty minutes.'

I was waiting outside, being blown to freaking bits by the wind. He opened the door of an Audi, urged me in. He had certainly dressed for the elements: a long Barbour coat, navy wool cap pulled to his ears. Now for the tricky part. I suggested we go to Blackrock, the area of beach passing on from the Salthill promenade. Before he could protest, I added,

'It's the best view and, trust me, buddy, no more awesome sight than the Atlantic at full roar. You up for that?'

Poking his pride.

He put the car in gear and we were speeding out of there. His face was stone. As we came off the Grattan Road, I saw the off-licence I'd been heavily dependent on still being there. I said,

'Kosta, stop a moment. Let's get some fortification for the wind.'

He pulled over, began to get out, asked,

'Jameson?'

'Perfect, and oh . . .' like I'd just thought of it, 'a pack of Gitanes.'

I didn't want them but I desperately wanted to buy time and prayed the assistant would have to go looking for such a brand, or at least explain why they didn't have them. I only needed minutes.

Four minutes and he was back, tossed over a pack of Marlboro, said,

'No Gitanes.'

The bottle of Jameson felt heavy as he handed it over. He glared at the sea, said,

'It's getting worse.'

He had no idea.

I said,

'Something you'll never forget.'

That clinched it.

He parked near the tower, the silhouette of the diving boards barely visible in the driving rain. I said,

'See under the tower, a shed. We can get protection there. When we were kids, we used to huddle under there, watch the sea roar.'

If kids had done it, how could he baulk? He sighed, reached in the glove compartment, took out the Glock, said,

'Force of habit.'

We made our way down along the side, the wind tugging like the worst kind of religion. Once inside the shed, we caught our breath, I unscrewed the Jay, handed the bottle over, said,

'This will warm you.'

He took a deep draw, handed it back, and I toasted,

'Long life.'

I used the Zippo to fire us up and he put the Glock on his knee, the charade at an end. He took but one long fervent pull of the cigarette and flicked it into the storm, asked,

'What's up, Jack?'

I said,

'I met your daughter.'

He was stunned, muttered,

'What?'

'Actually, she found me. Told me that Edward had many faults, but molestation wasn't one of them. She did say that he was chipping away at your business and you'd never allow that.'

He grabbed the bottle, drank, said,

'Poor girl, she's deluded.'

I let that sit, then,

'I checked around and, sure enough, he was no prince, but he wasn't what you said, and he was most definitely a rival to your business.'

He had the Glock in his hand, said,

'Spit it out, Jack.'

I did.

'You used me to erase him. That a friend of mine got killed was just friendly fire. Primarily, you got rid of a son-in-law you loathed.'

He stood up, watching the wild sea, said,

'Ah, Jack, why couldn't you just let it go?'

Levelled the gun at me, said,

'I liked you, Jack, I really did.'

Pulled the trigger three times and was bewildered, hitting

on empty. Now I stood, shucked the Mossberg free, said,

'I never wanted Gitanes, I just wanted time to, shall we say, de-fuse you.'

I racked the pump. He had to shout over the growing tempest,

'Jack, you're not going to do this. You owe me. I got rid of the priest and his playgirl housekeeper.'

I was taken aback but didn't lower the Mossberg. Gasped,

'Gabriel?'

He nodded, control sneaking back, said,

'See? I have your back, my friend. The priest was very cooperative; emptied all the bank accounts, too.'

Trying to keep my shock in check, I asked,

'He's dead?'

He waved a dismissive hand at the sky, said,

'He's in the wind.'

Then added,

'Which shows my friendship for you is real.'

I laughed, said,

'I love it, especially as you just attempted to unload a Glock into my face.'

I ordered,

'Give me the car keys.'

He did, his eyes darting round for an opening. I backed away, out of the shed. He asked,

'How do I get home without transport?'

I didn't look back as I climbed along the railing, said,

'Join Gabriel, go in the wind.'

30

The sacred and profane

Clancy, the Garda Superintendent, had been ominously absent during all of the Headstone drama. Didn't mean he didn't know.

How could he not?

Ridge becoming a media darling – he had to know my hand was in there. Mason, his new pet PI, taken off the board.

Once my best friend, he hated me with all the passion that once had bonded us.

The railway station where my dad had worked was being revamped. The staff were being moved to a new building in the wilderness close to the docks. An Irish Gulag. Did they have a say in this?

Right.

As homage to my father, I decided to take a last look at the station before they moved to the barren plains. I hoped I'd meet Brian Carpenter, for decades the station master, or Martin Quinn, who even as Mayor continued his day job on the railway. Now that's class.

As I got to the station, the members of the Simon Community were being sent out for the day, to kill time till they could return. One asked me politely if I could spare a cig and I gave him the packet. I moved on to the platform, could almost feel my dad's hand in mine as he showed me the trains when I was little more than a toddler.

Engulfed in memories of him, I failed to notice the burly figure come up behind me until he touched my shoulder. A train was approaching and I still wonder: if I hadn't moved as fast, would the touch have become a push?

I swirled round to face O'Brien, Clancy's hatchet man. We had bad history, mostly of violence and hurleys. He was surprised at my sudden turn, recovered, said,

'The Super would like a word.'

Not negotiable.

That much I knew from previous history. I followed him out of the station, resisting the temptation to look back. My dad was in my heart, that was what counted. A sleek Mercedes was outside, the engine humming, another thug at the wheel. I got in the back, O'Brien following.

The five-minute journey to Mill Street and the Garda Headquarters was swift and silent. I had nothing to say to these hoodlums.

We moved quickly into the station and then Clancy's domain/office.

He was sitting behind a new mahogany desk, as vast as his ego. He seemed to have grown in girth to accessorize it. Dressed in full uniform, a riot of insignia pinned on the tunic, he busied himself with papers as O'Brien took up position behind him, smirk in place. Finally he looked up, took off his gold pince-nez, said,

'Ah, the fingerless Taylor.'

I said,

'Nice to see you too. Sir.'

He gave a predatory smile as he pulled up a very old file, blew the dust dramatically off it, said,

'Jacko, Jack, you must be very proud, your dyke lady being promoted and your dope-dealer friend involved in the head shops.'

Stick it to him or not?

I stuck it, said,

'One does what little one can, as you know. The little, I mean.'

O'Brien moved but Clancy waved a restraining hand. He had better fodder than a wallop. Asked,

'You a fan of TV, Jacky boy?'

'Just TG4, the Irish channel.'

He was delighted, said,

'I think even they show a very popular series titled *Cold Cases*. We, in our own small way, have been going through old files, clearing the debris of the past, moving onwards and upwards to a new proud Irish nation.'

I was lost.

He tapped the file, said,

'This is your old man. Now, I liked your father. Such simple men seemed to be the very backbone of our society then.'

Seemed.

Very worrying.

He continued,

'But I hate hypocrites and I detest thieves.'

I tried with all my might to rein it in. O'Brien knew, waited till I moved and he could beat me senseless. Clancy continued,

'The files from the railway were fascinating, the pension fund especially. Did you know your father was in charge of it?'

I didn't.

He was cruising, killing me, pushed for the home run, said,

'He was a thief, stole from the very families he was supposed to be looking out for. And you, you've turned out just like him. He'd be very proud of the drunken, limping, deaf disaster you've become.'

Instinctively, I reached for the Walther in my waistband and O'Brien's face registered alarm, knowing he couldn't get to me in time. But there was no weapon. Out of respect to my dad, I'd left it at home. I let my hand show.

Empty.

Like the damn poem.

Empty of all

But memories of you.

I managed to mutter,

'Anything else, sir?'

Clancy looked to O'Brien.

The fuck was going on?

They'd hit me every which way but loose and I was . . . doing . . . nothing. O'Brien gave a cautious shrug and Clancy said, less certain now,

'No. You can go, but bear in mind, we'll be publicizing your father's thievery.'

I managed to turn around, moved to the door, stopped, said,

'My left hand still has its fingers.'

He was puzzled, asked,

'So?'

I lifted the middle finger, said,

'Cold case that.'

Reeling down the town, my mind on hyper drive from the revelations, I was stopped by a tinker woman who said,

'Jack Taylor.'

I nodded and she asked,

'My poor mother, she's dead three years now and I can't afford a headstone.'

I handed her my wallet, said,

'We can't have that.'

London Boulevard
Ken Bruen

Fresh out of prison, Mitchell is looking for a fresh start. Until he finds himself caught up with Robert Gant, a ruthless lowlife with violent plans.

To stay out of Gant's way, Mitchell takes work at the mansion of a faded movie actress. As she plies him with cash, cars and sex, he starts to wonder if this job comes with a catch.

But soon, Mitchell's past catches up with him. And when people close to him start getting hurt, he's forced to act, and take brutal revenge . . .

'Unnervingly clever'
NEW YORK TIMES

'Truly great entertainment . . . dark and disturbing'
TIME OUT

'Nastily entertaining'
THE BIG ISSUE

NOW A MAJOR MOTION PICTURE

Blitz
Ken Bruen

The Cop

Detective Sergeant Brant is tough and uncompromising, as sleazy and ruthless as the villains he's out to get. His violent methods may be questionable but Brant always gets results.

The Killer

Now, a psychopath has starting a killing spree across London. Calling himself 'The Blitz', his weapon of choice is a workman's hammer. And his victims are all cops.

The Target

The police squad are desperate to catch the killer before he catches up with them. And Brant is top of his list . . .

'Bruen writes tight, urgent, powerful prose'
THE TIMES

'Bruen is a distinctive talent . . . powerful, original
and controversial'
GUARDIAN

NOW A MAJOR MOTION PICTURE

Priest
Ken Bruen

Fresh out of hospital and back on the wagon once more, a new life beckons for troubled PI Jack Taylor.

Then Father Joyce is decapitated in a Galway confessional, shocking even the most hardened cynics and Taylor is asked to find his killer.

But Ireland is modernising quickly – too quickly Taylor thinks – and the church is rocked by scandal. Soon he is drawn into a dark web of murderous conspiracies.

What he cannot know is that the real danger is much closer and far more personal than he can imagine . . .

'Grimy, brooding, pawkily funny
and wholly original. Great'
OBSERVER

Sanctuary
Ken Bruen

Two guards; one nun; one judge.

When a letter containing a list of victims arrives in the post, PI Jack Taylor is sickened, but tells himself the list has nothing to do with him. He has enough to do just staying sane.

A guard and then a judge die in mysterious circumstances. But it is not until a child is added to the list that Taylor determines to find the identity of the killer, and stop them at any cost.

What he doesn't know is that his relationship with the killer is far closer than he thinks. And that it's about to become deeply personal.

Spiked with dark humour, and fuelled by rage at man's inhumanity to man, this is crime-writing at its darkest and most original.

'You don't want to meet Jack Taylor in person, ever, but if you're a big crime fan, you do want to read every book he features in'
IRISH TIMES

The Devil
Ken Bruen

America – the land of opportunity, a place where economic prosperity beckons – but not for PI Jack Taylor, who's just been refused entry.

Jack resumes his old life in Galway. But when he's called to investigate the frenzied murder of a student, he remembers an encounter with an over-friendly stranger in the airport bar. A stranger who seemed to know rather more than he should about Jack.

After several more murders and too many encounters to be coincidental, Jack believes he may have met his nemesis.

But why has he been chosen? And could he really be dealing with the Devil himself?

'Brilliant . . . once again he has delivered a disturbing story
that casts a very cold eye on the state of our nation'
IRISH INDEPENDENT